W9-AZB-721

The Numbers Game

That evening after supper Tom went to sit on the Reagans' front porch with Polly. I showed Papa my list and explained that I couldn't figure it out.

"You must do it by elimination," Papa said, "and you must start with the three squares in the middle. The rest is just a matter of getting two more combinations on the top and bottom to give you the answer."

It sounded simple enough. I went to the dining room so I could use the table. But by bedtime I still hadn't solved the puzzle. No wonder Tom was willing to risk fifty cents against a dime. Without the combinations Papa had given me, a fellow would have as much chance of solving the puzzle as a rooster does of laying an egg.

The next morning I told Tom I still hadn't been able to solve the puzzle.

"I think you're pulling a fast one on everybody," I told him.

"What do you mean by that?" Tom asked.

"I don't think it can be done," I said. "And after driving everybody crazy for a couple of days, you'll laugh about it like all get out."

"The puzzle can be solved all right," Tom said. "Tonight after supper I'll show you and the other fellows."

READ ALL THE BOOKS
IN THE GREAT BRAIN SERIES

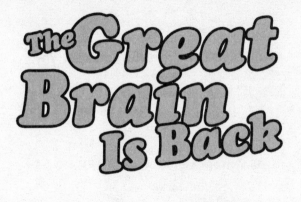

The Great Brain Is Back

JOHN D. FITZGERALD

Illustrated by Diane de Groat

PUFFIN BOOKS

For Edward Thomas, Jay Thomas,
Elise Christine, and Marianne Joy

PUFFIN BOOKS
An imprint of Penguin Random House LLC
375 Hudson Street
New York, New York 10014

First published in the United States of America
by Dial Books for Young Readers,
a division of Penguin Young Readers Group, 1995
Published by Puffin Books, an imprint of Penguin Random House LLC, 2017

Text copyright © 1995 by the Estate of John D. Fitzgerald
Illustrations copyright © 1995 by Diane deGroat

Penguin supports copyright. Copyright fuels creativity, encourages diverse voices, promotes
free speech, and creates a vibrant culture. Thank you for buying an authorized edition of
this book and for complying with copyright laws by not reproducing, scanning, or
distributing any part of it in any form without permission. You are supporting writers and
allowing Penguin to continue to publish books for every reader.

THE LIBRARY OF CONGRESS HAS CATALOGED
THE DIAL BOOKS FOR YOUNG READERS EDITION AS FOLLOWS:
Fitzgerald, John Dennis.
The great brain is back / by John D. Fitzgerald.
Illustrated by Diane deGroat.
p. cm.
Summary: Although bedazzled by pretty Polly Reagan, a thirteen-year-old Tom Fitzgerald's
great brain and money-loving ways haven't changed a bit.
ISBN 9780803713468
[1. Humorous stories] I. deGroat, Diane, ill. II. Title.
PZ7.F57535Gv 1995 [Fic]—dc20 94-17433 CIP AC

Puffin Books ISBN 9780425288740

Printed in the United States of America

10 9 8 7 6 5 4 3 2 1

Contents

CHAPTER ONE

The Slippery Soap Deal

THINGS GOT SO DULL in Adenville, Utah, in 1899 that I didn't know what to do with myself. It was all Polly Reagan and Papa's fault. Polly had put a spell on my older brother Tom. He carried her books to school and spent any spare time he had with her. He even squandered his money buying Polly ice cream sodas at the drugstore.

When Tom turned thirteen, Papa decided it was time for him to earn his keep. Papa was editor and publisher of the *Adenville Weekly Advocate*, the town's only newspaper, and he also did all the printing for people in town. He made Tom work with him after school and on Saturdays. About the only time I saw Tom was during meals and when we did our homework.

I'll tell you, life sure was dull for me. Tom had a money-loving heart and a great brain that he used to swindle me and all the other kids in town. Until he turned thirteen, hardly a week had passed without Tom pulling off one of his swindles. Although I was the victim many times, Tom's conniving ways had made life interesting and exciting.

Of course, I still had our little brother, Frankie. Papa and Mamma had adopted him when his parents were killed in a landslide. But Frankie was only six years old. I was eleven and too old to play with him. Sometimes I missed Tom so much that I felt like bawling.

I was sitting on the back porch steps one Sunday afternoon, wondering if life would ever be exciting again, when Tom came out of the kitchen and sat down beside me.

"Why aren't you over at Polly's?" I asked.

"She's at her grandmother's house," he said. "I'll be by Reagans' later," he added with a grin on his freckled face.

Tom was the only one in our family who had freckles. I took after Papa and had dark curly hair. My oldest brother, Sweyn, who was going to high school back east, was blond like our Danish mother. Tom was a mixture of Papa and Mamma. It was easy to tell Frankie wasn't a Fitzgerald because he had the straightest black hair of any kid in town.

Tom put his arm around my shoulders. "I've got a business proposition for you, J.D.," he said. We usually called each other by the initials of our first and second names because that was how Papa addressed us. We all had the same middle name of Dennis because it was a tradition in our family.

4

Every time Tom had put his arm around my shoulders and started talking about a business proposition, I'd lost money. But things had been so darn dull that I didn't have to think twice before answering.

"It's a deal," I said.

"But I haven't even told you what the proposition is yet."

"I don't care what it is," I said. "I'll take it."

I know that sounds crazy but I really didn't care if I lost my shirt. I was so happy Tom was back in business that I didn't care. At least there would be a little excitement.

"You will have to invest some money," Tom said, "but I'll guarantee you'll make a profit if you are any kind of a salesman."

"I'll do it," I said. "What's the deal?"

"Well, J.D., as you know, Papa only pays me fifty cents a week."

"The way Papa talks you'd think he was paying you seven dollars and a half a week," I said.

"Papa says room and board is worth a dollar a day, which is what Jimmie Peterson's mother charges at her boarding-house," Tom said. "That is why Papa claims he is actually paying me seven fifty a week."

"I'll sure hate to turn thirteen," I said, "and have Papa put me to work to earn my room and board."

"He says all boys should start earning their keep when they are thirteen," Tom said. "I can't argue about that. Practically every kid in town who is thirteen or older has some kind of a job or works for his parents. But it sure is tough on my pocketbook. I haven't been able to save a dime since I started working for Papa."

"If you hadn't bought Polly Reagan that ice cream soda last Saturday, you'd have some money," I said, to let him

5

know I'd never forgive him for falling under the spell of a girl.

"Forget about Polly," Tom said. "Let's get down to business. I saw this advertisement and it looked like an easy way to make some money. You buy fifty bars of soap at a nickel a bar and you sell the soap for ten cents a bar. That gives you a profit of two dollars and fifty cents. But I don't have time to sell the soap, so I'm willing to take a small profit and turn the whole deal over to you."

I made a noise in my throat to let Tom know I was thinking about his proposition and put my little brain to work.

Adenville had a population of about twenty-five hundred people: about two thousand Mormons, four hundred Protestants, and only about a hundred of us Catholics. There were a lot of places of business and homes west of the railroad tracks. East of the tracks were two saloons, the Sheepmen's Hotel, the Palace Cafe, a livery stable, a rooming house, and a few houses where poor people lived. With all those businesses and houses, selling soap was a peach of an idea.

"How small a profit?" I asked Tom when I was finished with all my thinking.

"Well," Tom said, "since it was my idea and you would never have had the chance to participate in this business venture if it wasn't for me, I'll turn the fifty bars of soap over to you for three dollars and a half. That will leave you a profit of a dollar and a half, when you sell the soap."

"Where is the soap?" I asked.

"I'm expecting it to arrive at the Express office at the depot this week," Tom said. "It is coming all the way from Chicago."

"I don't know," I told him. "I can find that advertisement and get fifty bars for two dollars and a half."

6

"No, you can't. I clipped the advertisement from the magazine. I'm giving you a chance to make a dollar and a half."

"I'll take it," I said, figuring a dollar and a half was a lot of money. Frankie and I only got twenty cents a week for doing the chores.

Tom dropped his arm from my shoulders and stood up. "All we need to complete this transaction," he said, "is for you to give me three dollars and a half from your bank."

We went up to our room. I got my bank and began shaking coins out of it.

"That is a lot of money," I said after I'd given Tom his three dollars and a half.

"Not as much as the five dollars you'll have when you sell the soap," Tom said.

"You made a dollar on the deal just answering the advertisement," I said, beginning to feel as if I'd been swindled.

"But if I hadn't answered the advertisement, you wouldn't have had the brains to do it," Tom said.

Tom picked up the soap at the depot on his way home from the newspaper office on Saturday. Papa had given him part of the day off because they were all caught up.

"You can use Frankie's wagon," Tom said. He helped me load soap onto the wagon. "Since you are now in business, J.D.," he told me, "you will need a pitch. Here is what you tell your customers. 'I'm selling Barker's All-Purpose Soap. It is the finest soap made and can be used for everything, including shampooing your hair.' Got that?"

I repeated the pitch. And suddenly I felt proud. Here I was in business for myself. I took two bars of soap.

"I'll try Mamma first," I said, and went inside to find her. Mamma was in the parlor with Aunt Bertha, polishing the furniture. She had a blue towel around her blond hair, and Aunt Bertha had a piece of brown cloth covering her gray hair. Aunt Bertha wasn't really our aunt. She had come to live with us after her husband had died because she didn't have any place to go. She was like one of the family.

"Mamma," I said.

"Later, John D.," she said. "Can't you see I'm busy?"

"This won't take long," I said. "I'm selling Barker's All-Purpose Soap. It is the finest soap made and can be used for everything, including shampooing your hair. It only costs ten cents a bar."

Mamma laid aside the furniture polish and the rag she had been using.

"Soap," she said as if it were a naughty word. "Where in the world did you get soap to sell?"

"Tom got it from an advertisement, and then I made a deal with him," I said. "I've got fifty bars to sell."

"At ten cents a bar?" Mamma said. "I can buy Cashmere Bouquet soap and several other brands for five cents a bar at the store."

"But not soap like this," I said, holding out a bar. "Just smell its fragrant odor. It came all the way from Chicago."

Mamma took the bar and smelled it. "I'll admit it has a nice odor," she said.

"You'll need one bar for the washbasin and one for the bathtub," I said.

"All right, John D.," she said. "I'll buy two bars, but that is all. And I'm only doing it because you are my son."

That sure wasn't saying much for my soap. But I collected twenty cents and went back outside. Tom was gone. Frankie was standing with his playmate, Eddie Huddle, staring at his wagon.

"What are you doing with my wagon?" he asked.

"I'm just borrowing it for a little while," I said.

"You got soap in it," Frankie said. "What are you doing with all that soap?"

"I'm going to sell it."

"Then you should pay me for using my wagon," he said.

I figured Frankie was entitled to something for me using his wagon. "I'll give you a nickel," I said.

"How much are you going to make selling that soap?" he asked.

"A dollar and a half," I said.

"Then I want a dime for my wagon," he said.

I couldn't carry the soap around. I needed the wagon. "All right," I agreed. "Here is your dime."

Frankie grabbed the dime. "Come on, Eddie," he shouted. "Let's go buy some candy."

I pulled the wagon around to the street. I decided to take all the houses on our street first, starting with Seth Smith's.

Mrs. Smith came to the front door after I rang the bell.

"Good afternoon, Mrs. Smith," I said. "I'm selling Barker's All-Purpose Soap. It is the finest soap made and can be used for everything, including shampooing your hair."

"How much is it?" she asked.

"Just ten cents a bar."

"That is mighty expensive for a bar of soap," she said.

"But this is a very special soap and comes all the way from Chicago," I said.

"I'll buy a bar, John," she said, "but only because you are our neighbor."

That sure as heck wasn't saying much for my soap. But I was convinced that when Mrs. Smith tried it, she would think it was the best soap she'd ever used.

I felt confident when I rang the next doorbell, at the Kay home. After all, Howard Kay was my best friend. When Mrs. Kay came to the door, I made my pitch.

"I'm sorry, John," she said, "but I don't need any soap."

"Soap won't spoil," I said. "You can keep it until you do need it. And don't forget, Howard is my best friend."

"When you put it that way," she said, "I suppose I'll have to buy a bar."

The next house was where the Bronson family lived. Mrs. Bronson answered the door. I made my pitch.

"I'm sorry," she said, "but ten cents is too much to pay for any soap." Then she shut the door.

Things got tough for me starting with Mrs. Bronson. People said the soap was too expensive or they didn't need any or they just plain didn't want it. I'd sold only seven bars including the two to Mamma when it was time to go home and do the evening chores.

I was beginning to believe The Great Brain had swindled me, but I didn't want to give him the satisfaction of knowing. When he asked me how the soap sales were after supper, I told him I couldn't complain.

The next day was Sunday. We always ate dinner at one o'clock on Sunday. Right after eating, I started out with Frankie's wagon and the soap. By the time I had to go home to do the evening chores, I'd sold only two bars.

Monday and Tuesday after school I covered all the rest of the houses on the west side of town and still had thirty-nine bars of soap. I was now positive that Tom had pulled another one of his fast deals on me. Most of the women said the soap was too expensive because they could buy soap for five cents a bar at the Z.C.M.I. store. Zion's Cooperative

Mercantile Institution was a long name for a store owned by the Mormon church. They had a store in every town and sold everything from shoelaces to plows. They had half a dozen kinds of hand soap for five cents a bar.

I knew I could sell the soap at five cents a bar. But if I did, I'd lose money on account of the three dollars and fifty cents I'd paid Tom. Not only that, it would make the eleven people who had paid ten cents a bar mad at me.

Wednesday after school I went across the tracks to the east side of town. I sold one bar to Mrs. Kokovinis, who owned the Palace Cafe with her husband. I think she bought it only because she knew her son, Basil, was a friend of mine. I even went to the back doors of the two saloons. The proprietors each bought a bar of soap, probably to get rid of me.

I was plumb down in the dumps when I stopped in front of the Sheepmen's Hotel. I sat down in the wagon beside the carton of soap. I had thirty-six bars of soap left and knew I couldn't sell them. Once again Tom had made me the victim of one of his swindles. Why, oh, why was I so dumb? I should wash my mouth out with soap for agreeing to the deal. Better still I should eat a bar of soap for being such a dumbbell.

I felt so sorry for myself that tears came to my eyes and I began to bawl. I'd made a dollar and forty cents selling soap. I had to give Frankie a dime of that. I'd paid Tom three dollars and a half. That meant I was out two dollars and twenty cents.

"What is the matter, John?" Mr. Prichard, the owner of the Sheepmen's Hotel, asked.

I hadn't seen him come out of the hotel. I looked up and quickly wiped the tears from my eyes with my sleeve.

"Nothing," I said.

"There must be something wrong to make you cry."

"I'm crying because I'm so dumb," I told him. "I'm so dumb I make a donkey look like a wise man."

Although I didn't think it was funny, because it was true, Mr. Prichard laughed. "Now, John, don't be so hard on yourself," he said. "What are you doing with all that soap?"

Mr. Prichard seemed so sympathetic and nice that I told him how Tom had swindled me, and how dumb I was to let it happen.

"Well, John," he said when I finished, "you said you have tried to sell soap to everybody in town, but that is wrong. You didn't try me. Is the soap any good?"

"It is supposed to be," I said. "I never tried it."

He picked up a bar of the soap. "Suppose we find out," he said.

I followed him into the hotel lobby and from there to the men's rest room. He took the wrapper off the soap and began washing his hands.

"It makes a good lather," he said. Then he held up his hands and inhaled. "It smells nice too. Not too strong a scent and not too weak. Seems like a good bar of soap to me."

He rinsed off his hands and left the bar on the washbasin. At least I'd sell one more. Mr. Prichard couldn't very well ask me to take it back after using it.

"Tell you what I'm going to do, John," he said. "I'll take the soap off your hands. I can use it here in the hotel."

I had sudden visions of becoming the king of soap salesmen, selling Mr. Prichard soap for his hotel.

"I can get more," I said. "Lots more."

"No, John," he said. "I buy my soap wholesale for less than half the price of this soap. It just happens the house-keeper forgot to order some and we are a little short. This

13

will have to be a one-shot deal."

I didn't know if Mr. Prichard was buying the soap just because he felt sorry for me or if he was telling the truth. Anyway, I wasn't going to argue with him. We went out and got the box of soap. Mr. Prichard had the desk clerk give me three dollars and sixty cents. I thanked him and went home.

I could hardly wait to let Tom know his swindle had backfired. He didn't say a word about soap during supper, but Mamma did as we ate dessert.

"Did you sell all your soap?" she asked. "I noticed you didn't bring any home with you."

I swallowed a mouthful of apple pie. "It is all sold," I said.

"At ten cents a bar?" Mamma asked. I nodded.

Then I looked across the table at Tom. He was so surprised, he was holding his fork with a piece of apple pie between his mouth and the table.

"You mean to tell me you sold all fifty bars of that soap at ten cents a bar?" he asked.

"Every last one," I said, really enjoying his astonishment.

"Well, I'll be a monkey's uncle," he said.

"I'm glad to hear you admit it," I told him.

That shut him up until we were doing our homework on the dining room table after supper.

"I was just thinking, J.D.," he said, "since you are such a super salesman, maybe I'd better order another case of soap."

I'd been waiting all of my life to turn the tables on Tom and his great brain.

"Go ahead and order another case if you want," I said.

"I'll make out the order right now," he said.

A week passed before the soap arrived. Tom gave me that old business of arm around the shoulders as we sat on the back porch steps with the case of soap in Frankie's wagon.

"Same deal as before. Right, partner?" Tom said. "You give me three dollars and fifty cents and the soap is all yours."

"No deal," I said.

"But you told me to order another case," Tom protested.

"I told you to order another case if you wanted to," I said. "I didn't tell you to order another case for me."

"But you made a dollar and a half on the last deal. How can you turn this deal down?"

"Easy," I said. "I don't want any part of it. It is your soap and you sell it if you can."

"If you can sell fifty bars with your little brain," Tom said, and was he ever angry, "I know I could sell a hundred with my great brain."

"You'll soon find out it takes more than a great brain to sell soap for a dime a bar when the Z.C.M.I. sells it for a nickel a bar," I said.

"I'll ask Papa to give me Saturday off," Tom said, "and I'll bet I sell all fifty bars during the weekend."

"How much do you want to bet?" I asked.

"You seem so darned sure of yourself," Tom said. "Do you swear on your word of honor that you sold all fifty bars of that soap for ten cents a bar?"

"I swear on my word of honor," I said.

"Then I'll just bet you fifty cents that I sell all fifty bars of this order," Tom said.

"It's a bet," I said.

15

Papa gave Tom Saturday off. When he came home at noon for lunch, he looked as if he'd lost a ball game.

"I don't know how you did it, J.D.," he said, "but everybody says a dime is too much to pay for a bar of soap. I didn't sell a single bar."

"Maybe I'm just a better salesman than you are," I said, really enjoying having put one over on him.

"Only one thing to do," Tom said. "I'll sell it for a nickel a bar. That way I'll get my money back."

Of course Tom didn't have any trouble selling the soap for a nickel a bar. He sold the fifty bars at five cents a bar that Saturday afternoon and the following afternoon. He looked tired when he came home just as Frankie and I were getting ready to do the chores. I couldn't resist rubbing salt in his wounds.

"You worked all day yesterday and this afternoon for nothing," I said. "I guess that proves you don't have such a great brain after all."

"You put one over on me, J.D.," he admitted.

"How does it feel to be on the receiving end of a swindle?" I asked.

"It wasn't a total loss," he said. "I sold all the soap and you owe me fifty cents."

"Wait a minute," I told him. "You didn't sell the soap for a dime a bar."

"That wasn't the bet," Tom said. "I bet you fifty cents that I'd sell fifty bars of soap, and I did. Let's go up to our room so you can give me the fifty cents from your bank right now."

Boy, oh, boy, what a dumbbell I was for betting. All my life I'd waited to put one over on Tom and when I did I had to open my big mouth and bet.

We went upstairs and I gave him fifty cents from my bank.

"You had better shake out some more money," Tom said. "You are going to need it."

"For what?" I asked.

"I called on some people you'd sold soap to for ten cents," Tom said. "I told them you'd made a mistake and should have charged only five cents. I told them you would be around to refund their money. If you don't, they will tell Papa and Mamma that you cheated them."

Boy, oh, boy, what a catastrophe that would be. I knew Papa and Mamma would insist I refund the money on the fourteen bars of soap. I congratulated myself that at least I'd sold thirty-six bars to Mr. Prichard, and Tom didn't know it. Then he caved the roof in on me.

"I was smart enough to know a hotel uses a lot of soap," he said. "So I went to see Mr. Prichard. He told me he'd bought thirty-six bars from you for ten cents a bar. I told him that was a mistake, and you'd be around to refund him the dollar and eighty cents you owe him."

"You did it just to get even with me," I said.

"You didn't think I was going to let you put one over on me and my great brain," Tom said. "I know Papa and Mamma will insist you refund the money so no one can say a Fitzgerald went around cheating people."

Not only would I lose all the money I'd made selling the soap, but I was also out the fifty cents I'd bet Tom and the ten cents I'd paid Frankie. I really was stupid as a donkey to think I could ever put one over on The Great Brain. You cannot fool a brother with a money-loving heart.

CHAPTER TWO

The Numbers Game

AFTER LOSING SO MUCH money on the slippery soap deal, I was ready for things to go back to being dull in Adenville, but it was too late. Tom had returned to his conniving ways.

It wasn't long before he began playing his silly numbers game. I thought the game was silly because he played it during his spare time, night and day. He got so interested in it that he didn't even go to sit with Polly Reagan on her front porch swing every evening.

I couldn't figure out what kind of game it was. I did know Tom used Frankie's blackboard, chalk, and eraser.

He'd take them and a notebook and a pencil up to his loft in the barn and just sit there writing down numbers on the blackboard and erasing them. He did the same thing in the parlor after supper.

One night Papa asked him, "What are you trying to do with all those numbers?"

Tom looked up from the blackboard he was holding on his knees. "A priest at the Catholic Academy told me one time about a magic square with numbers," he said. "I'm trying to figure it out."

Tom had gone for the seventh grade at the Jesuit Catholic Academy for Boys in Salt Lake City. That was before the Adenville Academy was built. Now Tom was an eighth-grader there.

"It must be some trick," Papa said. "You've been at it for three nights."

"And days," I said, remembering Tom working on the numbers while I dressed in the mornings.

"I know it can be done," Tom said, "because the priest said so. With my great brain, I'll figure it out."

Wednesday morning when I woke up, Tom had a big grin on his face.

"I did it," he said. "And now to make some money after all my hard work. J.D., when the kids are at Smith's vacant lot after school, you tell them to come to our barn after supper if they want to play the numbers game. Tell them it will cost them ten cents to win fifty cents. And tell them I'm taking twenty half dollars out of the bank before I go to work this afternoon."

"Some kids won't be able to come to our barn after

supper on a school night," I said. "That's when they finish their chores and homework."

"For fifty cents, they'll be there," Tom said. "Just you wait and see."

Seth Smith's father owned a big vacant lot that he allowed us kids to use as a playground. In return, we kept it cleared of weeds. There were about twenty fellows at the lot when I arrived that afternoon. When I said I had some important news, they all crowded around me.

"Tom says if you fellows want to play the numbers game to come to our barn after dinner tonight," I told them. "It costs ten cents to play, and you can win fifty cents."

Parley Benson pushed his coonskin cap to the back of his head. "Is this another swindle Tom is pulling?" he asked. Parley always wore his coonskin cap except when he went swimming.

Danny Forester's left eyelid flipped open. He had something the matter with that eyelid. It was always half closed unless he was angry or excited.

"Sounds fishy to me," he said.

Herbie Sties, who was a poet and as wide as he was high, spoke in rhyme.

"So Tom has got a numbers game
Another plan of his great brain.
It ain't strange and it ain't funny
He wants to swindle us out of our money."

"All I know is that Tom went to the bank to get twenty half dollars," I said. "That doesn't sound like a swindle to me."

Danny Forester put his face up close to mine. His eyelid

20

was back at half-mast. "You sure, J.D.?" he asked.

"Why don't you come to the barn and see for yourself?" I said.

Well, that did it. All the fellows decided to see if Tom really did have twenty half dollars. Most of them went right home to start their chores.

Every one of them showed up at our barn after dinner that night.

Tom was waiting outside the barn. He held up his hand and then counted the kids. There were nineteen of them, and I made twenty.

"I just wanted to make sure I had enough half dollars to pay if all of you happen to win the numbers game," Tom said. "Step right into the barn, fellows, and I'll explain the game to you."

After Tom said he'd been worried about having enough half dollars to pay everybody if they won, nobody wanted to be left out. We all trooped inside.

On the big wooden box that Tom had once used for a magic show was a stack of twenty half dollars. Next to it on an easel was Frankie's blackboard. On the blackboard was drawn the following:

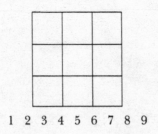

"Here is how you play the game," Tom said, pointing at the blackboard. "You can use each number only once. The idea is to place the numbers in the squares so they total fifteen across the squares, and fifteen from the top to the bottom of the squares, and fifteen from corner to corner from the left and the right. It is very simple. All you have to do is to find the right number to put in each square."

Tom picked up a notebook. "I have here a picture of the magic square and the numbers on a sheet of paper for each of you. J.D., pass them out."

I took the notebook and tore out a page for each of the fellows.

"Now," Tom said as he picked up another notebook and then pointed at a paper bag on the box. "Line up. As you pay your dime to play, I'll put it in the paper bag and write down your name in the notebook. Then I'll put in a half dollar for each player."

Parley Benson asked, "How much time do we have to figure the magic square out?"

"Today is Wednesday," Tom said. "You have until Friday after supper to figure it out. That is two whole days. You should be able to put the right numbers in the magic square by that time. *And*," he said, "to make it even better for you, you can get your parents to help if you want."

That did it. There wasn't a kid in the barn who didn't think he could figure the numbers game out in two days himself, let alone with the help of his parents. They couldn't wait to get in line and hand over their dimes to Tom. Tom put the dimes in the paper bag, along with a half dollar for each dime. Then he wrote down all the kids' names in his notebook.

23

I knew Tom had been working with those numbers for three days but that didn't stop me. It seemed so easy, only having nine numbers to put in the nine squares, that I got in line to play myself. Besides, I had an ace in the hole. Papa was a college graduate and would be able to figure out the magic square one, two, three.

After the other kids went home to finish their chores and do their homework, Tom went over to sit on the porch with Polly Reagan. I got my sheet of paper with the magic square and went to the parlor. I walked over to Papa.

"What have you got there, J.D.?" he asked, laying aside the magazine he'd been reading.

"The puzzle Tom calls the numbers game," I said. "The idea is to put the nine numbers in the nine squares so they total fifteen across and up and down and from corner to corner."

"So that is what T.D. was doing," Papa said. "Well, J.D., if you start out just trying to put numbers in the squares, you will have more than a thousand combinations. You have to do it by elimination. First you make a list of all the numbers from one through nine that total fifteen. For example, nine and one and five are fifteen. And nine and two and four are fifteen. Eight and two and five are fifteen. You have to list all the combinations that add up to fifteen."

"Then what?" I asked as Papa stopped talking.

"Then you have to keep trying the different combinations until you get the right answer," Papa said, "but it won't be easy because there are so many combinations, even when you eliminate those such as nine and three and three that use a number more than once."

I got my notebook and pencil and went into the dining room so I could write on the table. By bedtime, I had all the combinations, which looked like this:

```
 9   9   9   9        8   8   8   8   8   8
 1   5   2   4        1   6   2   5   3   4
+5  +1  +4  +2       +6  +1  +5  +2  +4  +3
15  15  15  15       15  15  15  15  15  15


 7   7   7   7        6   6   6   6   6   6
 2   6   3   5        1   8   2   7   4   5
+6  +2  +5  +3       +8  +1  +7  +2  +5  +4
15  15  15  15       15  15  15  15  15  15


         5   5   5   5   5   5   5   5
         1   9   2   8   3   7   6   4
        +9  +1  +8  +2  +7  +3  +4  +6
        15  15  15  15  15  15  15  15


 4   4   4   4   4   4        3   3   3   3
 2   9   3   8   6   5        4   8   5   7
+9  +2  +8  +3  +5  +6       +8  +4  +7  +5
15  15  15  15  15  15       15  15  15  15


 2   2   2   2   2   2        1   1   1   1
 9   4   8   5   7   6        9   5   8   6
+4  +9  +5  +8  +6  +7       +5  +9  +6  +8
15  15  15  15  15  15       15  15  15  15
```

As I looked at the numbers, I told myself that Tom's fifty cents was as good as mine. I was so excited that I stayed awake until Tom came to bed at nine. I showed him the list.

"Get your half dollar ready," I said. "I'm going to solve your puzzle."

"Saying it and doing it are two different things," Tom

told me. "But how did you figure out to do that?"

"Papa showed me," I said, "and you told us we could get our parents to help."

"I want you to do me a favor, J.D.," Tom said. "Don't tell anyone else about the combinations of fifteen."

"I'll show it to everybody and bankrupt you," I said, thinking of all the times Tom had swindled me and the other kids.

"There isn't another kid in town or his parents who have brains enough to figure out the combinations," Tom told me. "They will all go crazy trying to put numbers in the squares. But with the combinations some of them might accidentally hit on it. I'm asking you as a brother not to show anybody or tell anybody about the list."

What could I do after that "brother" business? I gave Tom my word of honor that I would keep mum.

Tom wasn't joking when he told me that saying I'd solve the puzzle and doing it were two different things. The next day during lunch and after school I worked and worked on the combinations, but I didn't get anywhere. I worked until Mamma reminded me it was time to go get a haircut and to take Frankie with me.

When we got to the barbershop, Danny's father, Mr. Forester, had a clipboard, a notebook, a pencil, and an eraser. He was sitting in the barber chair with the clipboard on his knees. I could see that a drawing of the magic square was fastened to it.

"There must be a thousand ways of putting these numbers in the squares," he said. "When Danny asked me about it, I thought it would be easy."

After we got our hair cut, Frankie and I stopped at the

Z.C.M.I. store to buy some candy. Mr. Harmon had a notebook and pencil and was trying to solve Tom's puzzle. I gave it another go when I got home, but had no luck.

That evening after supper Tom went to sit on the Reagans' front porch with Polly. I showed Papa my list and explained that I couldn't figure it out.

"You must do it by elimination," Papa said, "and you must start with the three squares in the middle. The rest is just a matter of getting two more combinations on the top and bottom to give you the answer."

It sounded simple enough. I went to the dining room so I could use the table. But by bedtime I still hadn't solved the puzzle. No wonder Tom was willing to risk fifty cents against a dime. Without the combinations Papa had given me, a fellow would have as much chance of solving the puzzle as a rooster does of laying an egg.

The next morning I told Tom I still hadn't been able to solve the puzzle.

"I think you're pulling a fast one on everybody," I told him.

"What do you mean by that?" Tom asked.

"I don't think it can be done," I said. "And after driving everybody crazy for a couple of days, you'll laugh about it like all get out."

"The puzzle can be solved all right," Tom said. "Tonight after supper I'll show you and the other fellows."

All the kids who had bet the numbers game were in the barn that evening. Tom arrived carrying Frankie's blackboard, a piece of chalk, and the bag of money. He stood behind the box.

"Did anybody win the numbers game?" he asked. "I'm ready to pay fifty cents to each winner."

Parley pushed his coonskin cap to the back of his head. "There ain't any winners and you know it," he said. "You've had your fun making fools out of us trying to solve a puzzle that can't be solved. Now, give us back our dimes."

"Just a minute, Parley," Tom said. "I'm going to show you the answer." He took the blackboard and drew the magic square. Then he put in the following numbers:

8	1	6
3	5	7
4	9	2

"You can see," Tom said, "that I've used only the numbers one through nine, each number once. You can add the numbers every which way and they total fifteen. So there you have the magic square, and you all lose, and I win."

Danny Forester's left eyelid flipped open. "I'll be a monkey's uncle," he said. "My pa said it couldn't be done."

"Anything is possible if you have a great brain," Tom said.

Later, as Tom and I walked toward the house, he put his arm around my shoulder. "I appreciate your not telling the other fellows the combinations," he said. "I appreciate it so much I'm giving you back your dime."

I took the dime. "I knew the combinations and I still couldn't solve it," I said.

"That's because you didn't try hard enough," Tom said. "You gave up too quick."

"Even with your great brain, it took you three days," I pointed out.

"That's how I knew nobody else could solve it in two days," Tom said and laughed. "Now I am taking my windfall over to Polly Reagan's house and inviting her to the drugstore for an ice cream soda."

I watched him walk off, but I didn't try to follow. I could hardly believe that The Great Brain could persuade his money-loving heart to shell out good money for an ice cream soda for a girl. I decided it was all part of that dangerous age of thirteen.

CHAPTER THREE

Indians

AT THE SAME TIME that Tom was pulling his soap swindle on me and separating the other kids from their money with The Numbers Game, something happened near Adenville, Utah, that caused trouble between the Paiute Indians and their neighbors.

The Pa-Roos-Its band of Paiutes were on a reservation about ten miles from Adenville. The people of our town had never had any reason to be afraid of the Indians until Henry Martin bought a farm adjoining the reservation. He was an unfriendly man who didn't mix with the people of the town and gave the impression that all he wanted was to be left alone. But he was a white man, and that was enough to make some other white people take his word of honor above that of an Indian.

A month after Henry Martin bought his farm, he made a citizen's arrest of an Indian he accused of stealing a saddle. It was Martin's word against the Indian's, and the Paiute went to the penitentiary. A few weeks after the trial Henry Martin made a citizen's arrest of another Indian, whom he accused of stealing a pig. Again it was Martin's word against the Paiute's, and the Indian went to the penitentiary. By this time some of the citizens of Adenville were beginning to become suspicious of Mr. Martin.

The day that the second Paiute was found guilty, Papa and Tom arrived home for dinner early. I knew something was up, but we are never permitted to discuss ugly subjects during meals, so I had to wait until after dinner to learn what had happened.

Papa had covered the trial for the *Advocate*, and he had taken Tom out of school that afternoon to attend with him. "I thought Tom could learn something about how a newspaper story is developed and also learn about our justice system," he said after he'd told us about the trial. "But I'm afraid what Tom witnessed was an unfortunate example of how things can go wrong."

"You think the Indian was innocent," Mamma said.

"You know I am not a wagering man, Tena," Papa said, "but if I were, I'd bet money on it."

"Chief Rising Sun looked like a thundercloud when he left the courtroom," Tom said. "He spoke on the Indians' behalf, but since his English was so poor hardly anyone listened."

Papa made a sound like a horse snorting. "I'd like to see any white person there speak Paiute," he said, "or even try."

"What will happen now?" I asked.

"You will do your homework, J.D.," Papa said. "You too, T.D."

"I don't believe the Paiutes were stealing," Tom told me when we were back at the dining room table, our books and papers spread in front of us. "They never stole anything from the Peckhams when the Peckhams owned that farm."

"The Peckhams didn't have anything worth stealing," I said. The Peckhams had tried dry farming out that way, but went broke and had to leave. I don't know what Henry Martin had paid them for the farm, but it couldn't have been much.

"The Paiutes have never stolen from anybody else I know either," Tom said, staring me straight in the eye.

That reminded me that Tom was blood brother to the Pa-Roos-Its band, ever since the time he wrote a letter to President McKinley and helped to catch a dishonest Indian agent who was cheating them. So I hunched over my homework and kept my mouth shut. Besides, I didn't think the Indians were dishonest, and I didn't like Henry Martin at all. He was a man I never saw smile.

Things were pretty quiet for a few weeks. Then early one Sunday afternoon Mr. Martin drove into town in his buckboard with the new Indian agent, Mr. Haley. In the rear of the buckboard was Chief Rising Sun's nephew, whose English name was Running Bear. Running Bear was tied with rope at the ankles and feet.

My uncle, Mark Trainor, was our deputy sheriff and marshal. He and Sheriff Baker came out of the jail, which also served as Adenville's marshal's and sheriff's office.

Sheriff Baker shook his head sadly. "Another one?" he

said. Although the light was at his back, he squinted his blue eyes at Mr. Martin.

Mr. Martin got down from the buckboard. "Caught him cold trying to steal my rifle," he said. "I started out for town this morning to get supplies. Got a mile or so down the road and found I'd left my list behind. I got back to the house in time to see this no-good Indian come out of my cabin with my rifle. I surprised him with my revolver and made him drop the rifle. Then I tied him up and took him to the reservation to get Haley."

Sheriff Baker looked at the Indian agent. "Any evidence besides Martin's word?"

Mr. Martin thrust his head into the sheriff's face. "You doubtin' my word?" he demanded.

"No," Sheriff Baker said, "but it does seem strange that we never had any trouble with the Paiutes until you bought that farm."

"Come out and see for yourself," Mr. Martin said. "It rained last night, and you can see this Indian's moccasin tracks going right up to my cabin and mud on the floor leading to my gun rack."

Sheriff Baker locked Running Bear in a cell, then got his horse. He accompanied Mr. Martin and Mr. Haley to the Martin farm.

Mr. Martin pointed. "You can see the Indian's moccasin tracks coming from the direction of the reservation and right across my yard to the door of my cabin. And you can see the tracks he made when leaving until I stopped him in the middle of the yard. Come closer. You can even see the imprint of the rifle in the mud when I made him drop it. Now let's go into the cabin."

They walked inside the cabin. Tracks from the muddy

moccasins ran from the door to the gun rack and back to the door.

"Satisfied, Sheriff?" Mr. Martin asked.

"Reckon so," Sheriff Baker said.

While this was going on, Tom and Papa paid a call on Uncle Mark and heard about Mr. Martin's latest accusation. "What does Running Bear say about what happened?" Papa asked. "As I recall, he was educated in the reservation mission school and speaks English." He had a pad and pencil out and was making notes to use in his story for the *Advocate*.

"Nothing," Uncle Mark said. "Before I put him in the cell, Running Bear told me that he didn't steal the rifle. Then he said, 'No white man will believe me, and white man's word is law.' Later I asked him if he wanted a blanket or anything else, but he didn't answer. He just stared at the wall."

"He'll talk to me," Tom said. "I'm a blood brother of the Pa-Roos-Its band." Then Tom went to the cell where Running Bear was held.

The brave sat cross-legged on the floor of the cell, his eyes fixed on the wall not three feet from his face.

"Running Bear," Tom said. "You know me. The great Chief Tav-Whad-Im made me a blood brother of the tribe." Tav-Whad-Im is Paiute and means Rising Sun in English. "I don't believe you stole the rifle. What happened?"

Running Bear didn't answer. He didn't take his eyes off the wall either. He sat there in the dark cell as if he'd been carved from stone.

Tom tried several times to get the Paiute brave to speak to him, but Running Bear would not speak nor move a muscle.

"This is bad," Tom said when he went back to the office

with Papa and Uncle Mark. "Running Bear won't even talk to me."

Uncle Mark pushed his Stetson to the back of his head. "I tell you, Running Bear has me worried," he said. "When an Indian acts like that, it sometimes means he has decided to give up the ghost. If he won't eat, he'll end up dead, and that will mean big trouble."

Papa and Tom stayed at the jail until Sheriff Baker came back to tell them what he saw at Martin's farm. While he was talking about it, Chief Rising Sun and a couple of braves rode into town. Chief Rising Sun asked to see his nephew.

Running Bear would not speak to the chief, nor would he look at him. When the chief left the jail and mounted his horse, there was a stern expression on his face.

"Then what happened?" I asked Tom that evening when he told me all about it.

"The Chief said that if Running Bear dies, there will be an Indian uprising," Tom said.

That made the hair stand up on the back of my neck. I'd never been anywhere near an Indian uprising, and I sure didn't want to be. On the other hand, I couldn't blame the Paiutes for fighting if their people were shut up in prisons to die. Especially if they hadn't done anything wrong.

"What's the matter, J.D.?" Tom asked when he noticed the expression on my face.

I didn't want to seem lily-livered, but I thought Tom would understand. "The whole idea of an Indian uprising scares the daylights out of me," I told him.

Tom nodded soberly. "Anybody would be scared," he said, "if they had the sense they were born with."

"How long does it take for someone to starve?" I asked.

"About four weeks," said Tom. Then he added, "It's about three weeks until the circuit judge will show up to hold a trial. My great brain should come up with a solution before then."

The next day after school I stopped by the jail to see if Running Bear had said anything or eaten. When I arrived, Tom was in the sheriff's office.

"Papa sent me over for the *Advocate*," Tom told me. "He wants to know if anything new has happened to put in the newspaper."

"Nothing new yet," the sheriff said. "The brave hasn't moved a muscle since he first sat down on that floor. He hasn't had a bite to eat or a sip of water for over twenty-four hours."

"No water?" Tom said, and his skin got an ashy color.

"What does that mean?" I asked.

"Bad news," Tom said. "A person can live about four weeks without food—but only about three days without water."

That *was* bad news. In three more days Adenville could be the center of a bloody battle.

"Can we see him?" Tom asked.

The sheriff glanced at me, then eyed Tom up and down. "Can't see what harm it would do," he said.

We went to the back of the jail, where the cells were, and sure enough, there was Running Bear, staring at the wall.

"Running Bear," Tom said, but the Indian might as well have been deaf for all the notice he took.

"Sheriff Baker says you won't drink anything," Tom said. "It's been a whole day now. In only two more days without water, you will die."

If Running Bear cared about that, he gave no sign. He sat there, his legs crossed, his hands on his knees, his face turned to the wall. It was hard to believe he was still alive.

"Chief Tav-Whad-Im says if you die there will be an Indian uprising," Tom said. "Many innocent people will suffer."

There was no sign that Running Bear had heard.

"What will happen to your wife if you die and there is an uprising?" Tom asked. "And your little son and baby daughter?"

From where I was standing, I thought I saw the Paiute's shoulders stiffen, but I wasn't certain.

"No use talking to him," the sheriff said. "His mind's made up. He's on his way to the land of the spirits."

"Are you going to put that in the newspaper?" I asked Tom when we'd left the jail house.

"I guess it's up to Papa. It's not the kind of news people want to read."

It wasn't the kind they wanted to hear either. When I went over to Smith's vacant lot after stopping by my house and changing my clothes, the fellows weren't any happier than I was when I told them.

"I'll fight if I have to," Jimmie Peterson said.

But Parley said, "Running Bear is a good Indian. He taught me things about trapping and skinning that even my father didn't know." That was something, because Parley's dad was an animal bounty hunter. "Early on the very day he was arrested," Parley went on, "he showed me some of the pelts he'd collected. I'm not his blood brother, but I sure don't want him to die of thirst, or to be shut up in the penitentiary."

"Me either," I told him.

That night I asked Tom if his great brain had figured out a way to prove Running Bear's innocence.

"Not yet," he said. "But I will." Then he got his new cap that Mamma had bought that day at the Z.C.M.I. store and put it on.

"Are you going over to the jail?" I asked hopefully, thinking I'd tag along.

"No, I'm going to see Polly," Tom said.

"You'd think when we're all about to die in an Indian uprising you'd have better things to do than visit Polly," I observed.

Tom looked surprised. "Like what?"

"Like put your great brain to work preventing it," I said. "All the fellows are worried, even Parley Benson. Parley told me that Running Bear taught him all sorts of things about trapping. He even showed Parley some pelts the morning of his arrest."

That was when Tom got the look in his eyes that he sometimes does when his great brain is hard at work. Usually this means that I or the other kids should watch our pocketbooks, as we are about to lose some money. This time, however, Tom said, "Well, I just think I'll stop to see Parley on the way to the Reagans' house."

The Benson place is nowhere near Polly Reagan's house, but from the set of Tom's shoulders, I knew it was no use asking what he was up to talking with Parley. All I could do was hope that The Great Brain would figure out a way to get us out of this mess Henry Martin had gotten us into.

The next afternoon, when school had let out, I stopped at the jail on the way home. Most of the other kids headed that way instead of toward Smith's vacant lot. When we arrived, there were about a half dozen men standing around in front of the jail and several ladies too. There were also some students from the Adenville Academy.

I saw Parley near the front of the crowd. He told me that he had asked Sheriff Baker if he could talk with Running Bear, but the sheriff told him Running Bear was not on exhibition to the public and that we should all go home and behave ourselves.

"Why did Tom stop by to see you last night?" I asked Parley.

"He wanted to know about the pelts Running Bear had with him Sunday morning. Tom asked if there was any special reason he had shown them to me."

"Was there?" I asked.

"Running Bear had a silver fox. It isn't very often a trapper gets hold of one of those. I'd never even seen one before."

I tried to work this out with my little brain, but I couldn't understand why Tom was wasting his time visiting Parley to talk about trapping when all of us were one day closer to dying in an Indian uprising.

That was when Sheriff Baker came to the front door of the jail. "You folks all go home now," he said. "There's nothing to see here."

Tom, who had just arrived, spoke up. "I'm here to interview you, Sheriff," he said. "The *Advocate* is going to run a big news story on all the events of the past few days. We're hoping to have it in tomorrow's edition."

The sheriff took his Stetson off and scratched his head. "Well, I guess you'd better come on inside," he said.

Tom told me later what happened inside the jail. Sheriff Baker sighed and looked at him. "There's nothing new happening, son," he said. "Running Bear stares at the wall. He won't eat, he won't drink, and he won't talk. I'm ready to ask for a troop of cavalry to come to Adenville in case of an uprising."

"But he'll listen," Tom said, "and I have something that will open up his ears and maybe his mouth too."

"I doubt it," the sheriff said. "But at this point I'm willing to take a chance on anything."

"You won't regret this, Sheriff," Tom said as he followed the sheriff back to the cells.

Running Bear sat in exactly the same position he'd been in when he was put in the cell. He didn't look a bit different, not even thinner from not eating.

"It is Tom, blood brother to the Pa-Roos-Its," Tom said. "I know Running Bear is on his way to the land of the spirits, but I wish him to delay his journey to listen to me. I have figured out what happened between you and Mr. Martin. If I am correct, Running Bear can live free and there will be no trouble between our friends, the Paiutes, and the people of Adenville."

Running Bear looked as if he hadn't heard a word.

"I am going to tell you what I believe happened," Tom went on. "If it is true, just nod your head, and we can prove it. If not, we will go away and never bother you again in your journey to the land of the spirits."

Running Bear stared at the wall.

"Sunday morning you knew Parley would be out early checking his traps," Tom said. "You had some pelts that were ready to trade, but before you traded them, you wanted to show him the pelt of the silver fox, since Parley had never seen one."

Running Bear gave no sign he'd heard.

41

"On the way back to the reservation, you met up with Henry Martin. He saw the silver fox and told you he would give you more for your pelts than you would get at the Indian Trading Post. So you went back with Mr. Martin to his cabin."

Tom paused, but the brave in the cell seemed not to notice.

"Mr. Martin told you he would trade you the rifle for the furs and that you should take it from the gun rack and leave. You left the cabin and he followed after you.

"When you had walked a little way from the cabin," Tom said, "Mr. Martin pulled his revolver on you and told you to drop the rifle. You did. Then he tied you up and took you to Mr. Haley and said he caught you stealing."

"Can you prove that, Tom?" the sheriff asked.

"Mr. Martin's bound to have that silver fox pelt in his cabin. It's worth too much to throw away, and he's no trapper, so we know he didn't catch it himself. Since Mr. Martin doesn't know Running Bear showed Parley the pelt a few hours earlier, he wouldn't figure it could be used as evidence against him."

"By jingo, you're right," the sheriff said.

The brave in the cell still hadn't moved a muscle. "Running Bear?" Tom said.

Slowly, Running Bear turned his head toward Tom. "Little brother speaks the truth," he said.

When the sheriff, Uncle Mark, Tom, and several other men from town went out to Mr. Martin's farm with a search warrant, they found the silver fox pelt hidden in his barn under several bales of hay.

"I trapped that myself," Mr. Martin said.

"Nobody but an Indian tans furs like these," Uncle Mark said. "The brave is innocent."

Mr. Martin's face twisted with rage. "Indians killed my woman and my son," he shouted. "Murdered them in cold blood!"

"And you think you'll get even by sending innocent people to prison," Uncle Mark said.

"An Indian's an Indian," Mr. Martin replied.

"An Indian is a human being like you or me," Uncle Mark said. "We are going to prosecute you for perjury."

And so it was Henry Martin who went on trial, and not Running Bear. Mr. Martin was like a crazy man. He kept screaming that all Indians should be put in jail, that it didn't matter that he'd lied, that he had a right to get even.

Running Bear returned to the reservation, and there was no Indian uprising. In time, the other two Indians were declared innocent also and returned to their homes.

The trouble between the citizens of Adenville and their neighbors, the Pa-Roos-Its band, was soon forgotten. But the Indians never forgot their blood brother and his great brain.

CHAPTER FOUR

The Great Bee

I NEVER KNEW just how strong a spell Polly Reagan had placed on Tom until The Great Bee took place in our town. That was when I almost gave up hope for my brother and his money-loving heart.

It was Mr. Monroe, the master at the Adenville Academy, who came up with the idea of having a giant spelling bee. The bee would involve all the kids at the Academy, which included seventh and eighth grade. That year there were thirty-two kids, counting Tom.

I first heard about the bee one night after supper. Tom and I had finished our homework at the dining room table. We went into the parlor, where Papa and Mamma and Aunt

Bertha were sitting. Papa was reading his weekly mail edition of the *New York World*, Mamma was embroidering flowers onto a pillowcase, and Aunt Bertha was darning socks. Frankie was playing with some marbles on the carpet. He'd used a piece of string to make a circle and was practicing using his new aggie shooter.

"There you are," Papa said when Tom and I came into the room. He folded his newspaper on his lap. "I had something to tell your mother and Aunt Bertha, but I felt since you were involved, T.D., I should wait until you finished your homework."

When Papa said Tom was involved, my heart sank. All I could think of was that one of his shenanigans had caught up with him again.

"As you know," Papa said, "Mayor Whitlock is chairman of the board of directors of the Adenville Academy."

This was worse than I had feared. I glanced sideways at Tom, but he just stood there watching Papa, as cool as a cucumber. Whatever Tom had been up to, he sure wasn't worried about it.

"Well, he came to see me today," Papa said. "He asked me if I would be the judge in a spelling bee."

I couldn't help it. I felt disappointed. At least when Tom was involved in one of his swindles, life was exciting for me and the other kids in Adenville. Spelling bees were hardly exciting at all. We had them all the time in the common school. Mr. Standish, our teacher, thought they were a good way to get the students interested in spelling.

"Why would Mr. Whitlock ask you to judge a spelling bee?" Tom asked.

"Because this is going to be the greatest spelling bee ever to take place in Adenville," Papa said. "Mr. Monroe went to

Mr. Whitlock and the rest of the school board and said he proposed to make the students at the Academy the finest spellers in all of Utah."

"My lands," Aunt Bertha said.

Mamma looked up from her embroidery.

"The school board asked different business people in town to donate prizes. A group of us went in together to pay for the first prize, which will be a brand-new bicycle."

Tom whistled.

"Second prize will be a ten-dollar gold piece, and third prize will be a certificate worth two dollars at the drugstore."

Now Papa had everybody's interest, mine included. "I don't see why us kids at the common school can't compete," I said. "It's not fair at all. The only prize we ever get in spelling is a gold star on our report card if we do perfect work all year."

Papa looked straight at me. "If I recall correctly, J.D.," he said, "you are in no danger of earning one."

I shut my mouth in a hurry.

"I sure could use a new bicycle," Tom said, and I could tell by the expression in his eyes that he was already planning how to get it.

"Will you mind if your father is the judge?" Papa asked.

Tom grinned. "Don't worry," he said. "When I win The Great Bee, nobody will think it's because you're the judge. They'll know it's because of my great brain."

"Which up until now hasn't been much interested in spelling," Papa said.

When Papa said that, I wondered if the whole idea really had been Mr. Monroe's. Papa said that now that Tom was helping to set type at the *Advocate*, finding spelling errors in the newspaper had become a sport in Adenville.

Papa made it sound as if Tom was the world's worst speller, which wasn't true at all. The fact was that Tom never was interested in studying spelling. He said he had more important things for his great brain to concern itself with. And even without studying, he hardly ever misspelled anything. Most years in common school he'd missed a gold star by only two or three words.

"Just to show you how important I think this contest is," Papa said, "I am going to give you an hour off work every day after school from now until the bee. That should give you plenty of time to prepare for the contest, which will be held two weeks from Saturday at the school."

Then Papa looked at me. "And, J.D.," he said, "one of your chores for the next two weeks will be to help Tom with his spelling drills."

I didn't think that was one bit fair since I couldn't enter The Great Bee, but nobody asked my opinion.

"First prize will be exhibited in the window of the Z.C.M.I. store until the day of the contest," Papa said. Then he went back to reading his paper.

"Papa is getting two people to learn spelling when only one of them can win the prize," I said to Tom later. "It's even too late for me to get a gold star on my report card since I've been missing spelling words all year."

"You might change your tune when I win that bicycle," Tom said. "After all, I'll be starting high school back east at the end of the summer. I won't be home after August to rent out my old bicycle, and somebody will have to use it."

"It still is in pretty good shape," I said. Sweyn had given me his old bicycle to use, but it had been ridden for so many

miles by so many different kids that I was always needing Tom's or Papa's help to repair it.

"I'll give you a fair price since you're my brother," Tom said. Then he went off, whistling, to see Polly Reagan.

The next day when school let out, the other fellows and I stopped by the front window of the Z.C.M.I. store before we went home. By the time we arrived, there was already a crowd of kids from the Academy, which lets out at the same time as the common school but is closer to the commercial district of Adenville.

Practically all the fellows from the Academy were there and most of the girls too. Even Andy Anderson, who could never ride a bicycle because of his peg leg, was looking in the window. Tom was right in front of the crowd, with Parley Benson on one side and Polly Reagan on the other.

When I managed to work my way through the crowd, I was right behind Tom and Polly. By standing on tiptoe, I could look over their shoulders and see the entire display. I could also see that Tom was carrying Polly's books while all she had in her hand was a fancy lunch bucket. I ignored them and looked in the window.

Much to my surprise, there were two bicycles in the window. One was a Waverley with a diamond frame painted bright red with black stripes, and a Bridgeport searchlight mounted on the handlebars. Beside it stood a drop-frame lady's bicycle in sky blue. The lady's bicycle had a warning bell instead of a searchlight. Both bicycles had cyclometers so the owner could tell how many miles had been ridden.

At first, two bicycles made me think there must be two first prizes being offered in The Great Bee, but Papa had mentioned only one prize. Then I noticed the sign in front of the bicycles. It said:

ONE OF THESE FINE BICYCLES
WILL BE THE FIRST PRIZE
IN THE GREAT SPELLING BEE.
A LUCKY BOY OR GIRL
WILL RIDE IN STYLE
BECAUSE OF SUPERIOR ABILITY
AND LOVE OF LEARNING.

THESE BICYCLES FEATURE SAGER CYCLE SADDLES AND
HARTFORD SINGLE-TUBE PNEUMATIC TIRES.

Parley Benson adjusted his coonskin cap. "That is one fine machine," he said. "I wouldn't mind owning it at all."

"Me either," Sammy Leeds added.

I looked at the man's bicycle and was overcome by jealousy of my brother Tom. First off, he was older than me, and then he had his great brain, and now he was going to win the spelling bee and own a fine new Waverley bicycle. Life sure wasn't fair.

"Well, fellows," Tom said. "Look all you want, but I am going to be riding that bicycle in two weeks."

"Oh, Tom," Polly said. "Why would you think such a thing?"

Tom looked at Polly. I wondered why he didn't notice me peering over their shoulders, but he didn't. "Because me and my great brain are going to win that bicycle," he told her.

"Goodness!" Polly said and laughed. "Everybody knows that I am the best speller around. Every single year we were in common school I took home a gold star on my report card for perfect spelling."

Tom had amazement written all over his freckled face.

"But why would you want to win the spelling bee?" he asked.

"To win the bicycle, of course." Polly had a little pink color on her cheeks.

"But you already have a bicycle," Tom said.

"It's a girl's bicycle," Polly said, "and it doesn't have a warning bell or a Sager saddle. That bicycle in the window is the most beautiful woman's bicycle I've ever seen, and I intend to win it at the spelling bee."

Because I was standing right behind them, I could see Tom's Adam's apple move up and down as he swallowed. He didn't say anything, though. That whole crowd of kids was so still that you could hear a pin drop.

Then Dotty Blake, who used to be called Britches Dotty before Tom taught her to read and Mamma made her some good clothes, spoke up.

"I don't see why anyone could ever want one of those contraptions," she said. "Not when they could ride a horse."

"You're just saying that because there's no way you could ever win at spelling," Sammy said. He had hated Dotty ever since she'd made him the only boy in Advenville ever to get beat up by a girl.

Dotty didn't answer Sammy. She just stared at him until Sammy looked away and started to whistle as if he didn't care what everyone in the crowd was thinking.

Herbie Sties spoke in rhyme, as usual.

"T.D.F. might win the bee
If it weren't for good old me.
I want that bicycle, sure as shootin'.
And I'm going to win it, you're darned tootin'."

Danny Forester's left eyelid flipped open farther than I'd ever seen it go before. "This Great Spelling Bee sure is one event I don't want to miss," he remarked. "It will be much more interesting than any fight I've ever seen in Smith's vacant lot."

I could hardly wait until we got home to rub salt in Tom's wounds.

"Polly Reagan sure is going to be mad at you," I said, "when you win that bicycle."

"Don't worry," Tom said. "My great brain will figure out a way to win that Waverley bicycle and to keep sitting on Polly's porch swing too. Now, here are the words I want you to drill me on today."

Boy, oh, boy. I looked at that list and it was just like being in school again. Worse, because I'd already spent practically the entire day in school, and after I'd finished my chores and supper, I'd still have homework to do.

The first word was *emporium*.

"*Emporium*," I said.

"*Emporium*," Tom said. "E-m-p-o-r-i-u-m. Emporium." Then he said, "You know, in the spelling bee, the person who gives out the word will use it in a sentence, but we'll skip that part."

"All right." I looked at the list. "Deuteronomy."

Tom spelled *Deuteronomy*.

"Why did you put that word on your list?" I asked. "That's a book in the Bible."

"Because Bishop Aden is one of the people submitting words."

"How do you know?"

"I asked Papa. Bishop Aden, Mr. Monroe, Mr. Standish, Reverend Holcomb, and Mr. Whitlock are making up a big list of words. Bishop Aden will give the words, Papa will judge the spelling, and Mr. Standish will keep the time."

Tom's great brain had already figured out what a lot of the spelling words would be. Well, that would be much easier than figuring out a way to win and to keep Polly happy too.

"Are they going to have a contest every year?" I asked, thinking that maybe my hours of drilling Tom wouldn't be wasted if that were so. The next year I'd be at Adenville Academy, and I'd have a head start in learning words.

"Just give me the words, J.D.," Tom said. "Most of my hour is already gone."

When Tom's hour was up, he took the list of words he'd given me, shoved it in his pants pocket, and went off to work for Papa at the *Advocate*.

I fed and watered our team of horses, the milk cow, and Dusty, Sweyn's mustang. Then, leaving the rest of my chores until after dinner, I hurried over to Smith's vacant lot.

Howard Kay and Jimmie Peterson were there. Jimmie had grown a lot during the school year, so for a change his clothes fit him. Most of the time they were a size too large. His mother bought them that way since he had no younger brothers to wear hand-me-downs. They were meant to last two years, so by the time Jimmie grew into them, they were worn out or only good for play clothes.

Howard and Jimmie were just standing around. Howard was kicking at the dust. Herbie Sties, Parley Benson, Seth Smith, and Danny Forester were sitting together under a tree.

"Where's Basil?" I asked.

"Did you forget?" Howard said. "Basil turned thirteen this week. His parents say he has to work with them in the Palace Cafe every day after school and on Saturdays too."

"Boy, oh, boy," I said. "The more I hear about thirteen, the less I want to be it."

"Sure is an unlucky number," Howard said.

I looked at the boys sitting under the tree. Herbie and Seth were both twelve and in the first year at the Adenville Academy, but Parley and Danny were thirteen.

"Why aren't you at work?" I asked Danny.

"I got off early," he told me.

I didn't bother to ask Parley why he wasn't at work. Parley helped his father tend traps, but that was mostly early in the morning before school.

"*Conscious*," Seth said. "Always let your conscious be your guide."

"That's *conscience*," I told him.

But Herbie said,

"I'll spell both words

and thus work towards

winning the bee

one, two, three!"

and he spelled the words correctly.

"*Champion*," Parley said to Danny. "I want to be spelling champion. *Champion*." Danny spelled it for him.

It sure was disappointing to come over to Smith's vacant lot and find the kids studying there too. The next couple of weeks were no fun at all. Life was so boring that it was hardly worth being a kid. When I wasn't drilling Tom on spelling, I was over at Smith's vacant lot listening to the other fellows drilling one another.

When Tom ran out of words from the Bible and the newspaper, he started making up lists of words from geography and history and all the other subjects kids study in school.

"*Paiute*," I said one afternoon three days before The Great Bee. "The Paiute Indians are our friends. *Paiute*."

"I told you that you don't have to use the word in a sentence," Tom said. Then he spelled *Paiute*.

"Can I have that list?" I asked when we were done, thinking ahead to next year.

"Sorry," Tom said as he folded the list and stuck it into his pants pocket, "but I need it."

He knew every word on that list. I was so curious as to what Tom was doing with it that I followed him over to Polly Reagan's after supper.

Tom rang the doorbell and went inside for a couple of minutes. Since it was a fine evening, he and Polly soon came out on the porch. By then I was hiding underneath it.

There were plenty of spiderwebs and dust under the porch, and there was also Polly's dog, One Spot. One Spot came over to lick my face. It was all I could do to keep quiet with that dog slobbering on me, but I sure didn't want Tom and Polly to catch me.

When One Spot quit licking me, I listened carefully and heard the sound of people eating. I raised my head and sniffed, same as One Spot. I could smell cookies.

"These are delicious," Tom said.

"Thank you," Polly said. "I made them before dinner."

One Spot was a lot luckier than I was. He went out from under the porch and up on top of it. Polly gave him a cookie.

"Now," Tom said. "*Paiute*."

"*Paiute*," Polly repeated, then spelled the word.

At first I could hardly believe my ears. Then I thought my brother had gone plumb loco. He went through that whole list of words. Then Polly started on a list she'd brought. I didn't listen to many of her words. It was all too much for my little brain. I crawled out from under the porch and went home.

Had all those spelling words done something to Tom's great brain? Or maybe it was Polly's spell. Maybe she'd turned his money-loving heart into one as soft and silly as Sweyn's when he started going with Marie Vinson, or Greg Larson's when he took up with Sally Anne Carver. All this only made me more certain that I wanted to try as hard as possible never to let a girl put a spell on me.

Mr. Whitlock and the other members of the school board decided that the Academy wouldn't be large enough to hold all the people who wanted to attend The Great Bee. Bishop Aden offered the use of the Mormon Church, or The Church of Jesus Christ of Latter-day Saints as the Mormons called it. There were so many Mormons in Adenville, their church was the biggest meeting hall in town.

The Great Bee was scheduled to begin at seven o'clock on Saturday night, but the best seats were filled by six-thirty. We were lucky Mamma had made an early dinner. Our family was only three rows from the small stage and the choir loft, where the thirty-two students participating in the contest sat.

The contestants were called onto the stage one at a time. For a long time nobody missed a word except for Tubby Ralston, who couldn't spell any better than I could. Then Seth Smith went down, and Frank Jenson. By nine o'clock there were only five contestants still on the stage. One was Parley, who wasn't wearing his coonskin cap. He looked kind of strange without it. I had forgotten how his hair stood up in cowlicks on top of his head.

Then Parley missed *omnipotent*, and Tom got it right. Now only Tom, Polly, Herbie Sties, and Danny Forester were still sitting in the choir loft. All of them were beginning to look tired, but they were also excited. There were three prizes and four contestants.

Then Danny Forester stood and walked onto the stage.

"*Emporium,*" Bishop Aden said. "An emporium is a store that carries general merchandise. *Emporium.*"

I figured Bishop Aden must have been running out of words as that one was easier than some of the others he'd given during the past half hour.

Danny must have thought so too. "*Emporium,*" he repeated quickly. "E-m-p-o-u-"

A sound like loud sighing went through the church, then muttering and conversation. Danny didn't have to wait until Papa judged the word misspelled. His shoulders slumped and he walked off the stage, down the aisle to the back of the building.

I sure felt sorry for Danny. All that hard work and excitement and at the very end of the contest he was out on his ear.

At least I thought it was the end of the contest. A whole half hour passed until another person missed a word. That person was Herbie and he missed *terrestrial.* Herbie didn't look particularly upset. He just clumped off the stage and down the aisle to sit with his folks. I figured Herbie probably didn't feel too bad, because he'd won two dollars' worth of merchandise at the drugstore. Two dollars can buy a lot of ice cream sodas, fudge, and candy.

Only two people were left, Tom and Polly. Instead of calling the next word, Bishop Aden went on the stage.

"Ladies and gentlemen," he said, "we are going to take a little break here to give our final contestants a chance to stretch and get themselves a drink of water." He smiled then and added, "Also, our board is going to have to come up with some more words because I've just about extinguished the list that was written for me."

Tom and Polly left the choir loft, but not everybody in the church did. I guess they must have been afraid of losing their seats. I didn't have to worry since Mamma was there to hold mine. I went outside and ran over to where Tom was standing with a couple of fellows.

"This is it, T.D.!" I shouted. "That bicycle is practically yours."

"Don't count on it, J.D.," Tom said. "Remember all of Polly's gold stars."

That wasn't all I remembered. I remembered Tom sitting on the Reagans' swing, going over his list of words with Polly. My spirits sank lower than a worm's belly, and I was sure that The Great Brain had gone soft at last. Polly's spell was about to make him give up the finest bicycle that Adenville had ever seen.

"You mean you're not going to win?" I asked, looking Tom square in the eye.

"Of course I am," Tom said. "I told you my great brain would find a way to keep everyone happy."

When I went back to my seat, I couldn't help thinking that there was no way this could happen. To make matters worse, somebody had put two chairs on the stage so Tom and Polly could sit there instead of in the choir loft. I, for one, was going to be deeply unhappy to see Tom humiliated in front of most all the citizens of Adenville.

Whoever came up with that new list put some real humdingers on it. The next word that Bishop Aden read was one I'd never even heard of: *lachrymose*. Polly stood, repeated it, and spelled it off as if she'd learned it in her cradle.

The same thing happened with Tom's word, *soliloquy*.

This went on for another forty minutes. By then both

58

Tom and Polly were looking white as sheets and completely worn out. Polly sat with her eyes on the stage floor until it was her turn each time, and Tom sat with his eyes on Polly except when he had to face the audience.

My hands started to hurt, and I looked down to see that they were tightly clenched into fists. I was relaxing them when Polly missed a word.

"*Mundi,*" Bishop Aden said. "*Sic transit gloria mundi. Mundi.*"

"That isn't even English," Mamma whispered next to me. "It's Latin."

I was glad to hear that because I'd been afraid my little brain had given out on me.

"*Mundi,*" said Polly. "M-o-n-d-i."

"Incorrect," Papa said. "You may take your seat."

Tom came forward and stood there while Bishop Aden repeated the word and then the sentence.

"*Mundi,*" Tom said.

I held my breath.

"M-u-n . . ." He paused.

I clenched my eyes tightly shut.

"d-a-e," Tom finished.

"Sit down," Papa said. "The word is spelled "M-u-n-d-i."

Then Bishop Aden said, "*Hyssop.*"

Both Tom and Polly got that, I guess from Tom's list of Bible words. They also got all the words for the next fifteen minutes.

That was when Mayor Whitlock went to the front of the stage. "Ladies and gentlemen," he said, "I have an announcement to make."

I don't know about anyone else, but I sure perked up at that. Was Mr. Whitlock going to call the contest because it was so late and there was church in the morning? Would it continue the next afternoon? Had Papa misjudged a word? All those thoughts crowded my little brain so that I could hardly take in what Mayor Whitlock said next.

"During the break about an hour ago, our panel came up with some new words," the mayor said, "most of which I couldn't spell myself."

At that point everybody laughed.

"And at that time we also decided should our two contestants finish that list, Adenville would have two spelling champions—"

That was when everybody started cheering. Some of the fellows threw their hats in the air. Parley's coonskin cap sailed over my head and landed at Mayor Whitlock's feet.

The mayor held his arm in the air until everyone got quiet again.

"Ladies and gentlemen," he said, and he turned to hold his hand toward Polly, and then toward Tom, "I give you the winners of the bicycles, the finest spellers in all of Adenville, Miss Polly Reagan and Mr. Thomas D. Fitzgerald."

The Great Brain had done it again. Tom had outsmarted everybody, kept his place on the Reagans' porch swing, and also won a brand-new Waverley bicycle.

I only wondered about one thing. I kept quiet about it until Tom and I were up in our bedroom at midnight, getting ready for bed.

"Did you misspell that word on purpose?" I asked.

"What word?" Tom asked, an innocent expression on his freckled face.

"*Mundi*," I said.

"Well, J.D.," Tom said. "That is for me and my great brain to know, and you and your little brain to find out."

CHAPTER FIVE

The Dogfights

I NEVER DID FIND OUT if Tom misspelled *mundi* on purpose. Something happened soon after school let out for the summer to make me forget all about The Great Bee.

When Tom and Papa appeared for supper one evening looking very subdued, I was afraid that Tom had been backsliding. For the life of me, I couldn't think of anything else to make Papa look so upset. I had to wait until after supper to find out what had happened.

Papa hadn't seemed to enjoy his meal very much, and he appeared weary as he walked over and sat down in his rocking chair. He clasped his hands on his knees until the blood veins stood out.

"A man named Bill Bartell is going to bring dogfighting to Adenville," he told us. "Bartell rented the old Kingston farm on the outskirts of town. He's going to build a pit in the barn and hold dogfights there."

Mamma's face became pale. "You mean the kind of dogfights where one dog kills the other one?" she asked.

"These dogfights can end two ways," Papa said. "One dog kills the other dog, or one dog is so chewed up it can't fight anymore."

"But can't Mark and Sheriff Baker put a stop to it?" Mamma asked.

"There is no law in Utah against dogfighting," Papa said, "although it's a brutal and inhumane sport. I once saw a dogfight in Silverlode before it became a ghost town, so I know firsthand."

"Maybe nobody will attend the fights," Mamma said hopefully.

"There are enough cowboys from ranches and other people who'll attend to make it a paying proposition for Bartell," Papa said. "I printed handbills for him today." Papa removed a folded piece of paper from his pocket and handed it to Mamma.

I saw the handbill after Mamma and Aunt Bertha read it. It stated:

• DOGFIGHTS •
BEGINNING JUNE 28TH
DOGFIGHTS WILL BE HELD IN THE KINGSTON BARN
AT THREE O'CLOCK
EVERY SATURDAY AFTERNOON.
ADMISSION $1.00

I looked at Papa. "How do they get dogs to fight until

one is killed or hurt so badly it can't fight anymore?" I asked.

"They are trained to kill," Papa said. "I didn't want to print that handbill, but I'm obligated to print anything a customer wants. Well, at least I'll see to it that Bartell doesn't get any publicity for his dogfights in the *Advocate*."

"Papa," Frankie said, tugging on Papa's sleeve. "Where does Mr. Bartell get the dogs from?"

"I don't rightly know," Papa told him, "but I suppose he picks up strays or even buys dogs and then trains them to fight. I've been told he brought six dogs with him. And in every town there are men who own dogs they consider to be good fighters. The proprietor of the Fairplay Saloon has a bulldog named John Bull that he considers the best fighter in town. You can bet he will want to match his dog against one owned by Bartell."

"I've seen John Bull in a fight," I said. "But he doesn't fight fair. He has that big collar on him. No wonder he can lick any other dog in town."

"The dog won't be wearing a collar if he's ever matched against one of Bartell's dogs," Papa said.

Mamma held up her hands. "Please don't talk about it," she said. "It makes me ill even to think about such a horrible thing. Dogs are supposed to be pets or watchdogs, not trained to kill one another."

That night I couldn't go to sleep. I was awake when Tom came up to bed an hour later.

"Can you figure out a way to stop those dogfights?" I asked.

"You heard Papa. Dogfights are legal in Utah," Tom said as he removed a shoe.

"You could put your great brain to work on it," I told him.

63

"I guess I'll have to," Tom said, "since the grown-ups don't seem to be able to do anything about it."

Tom and Papa had just finished a big printing job for the county the afternoon Papa found out about the dogfights.

"You can take a few days off," Papa told Tom the next morning at breakfast. "With that county job out of the way, I shouldn't need your help for a week or so."

Right after breakfast Tom went up to his loft in the barn to put his great brain to work on the dogfights. He came down just as Frankie and I finished the morning chores.

"Where are you going?" I asked.

"To do some scouting," he said.

"Can I come?" I asked.

"All right," Tom agreed, "but you'll have to do as I say."

Frankie stepped in front of Tom. "I want to come too," he said.

"You are too little, Frankie," Tom told him. "You stay and play with Eddie Huddle when he comes over."

Tom and I got our bikes. We rode to the outskirts of town. Then we hid the bikes in an apple orchard.

"We are going to spy on Mr. Bartell," Tom said. "We'll have to sneak up on the Kingston farm without being seen."

We went through cornfields, another orchard, and alfalfa fields until we were in back of the Kingston farm. There were no crops growing there, but the weeds were high enough for us to crawl under cover to the top of a small ridge. From the ridge we could see the farmhouse, the barn, and Mr. Bartell's wagon. His team of horses were in a fenced pasture.

We waited for what seemed like hours before we saw Mr. Bartell come out of the back door of the farmhouse. He began stretching as if he had just gotten up. Then he went to the barn. He unlocked the padlock on the door and entered. As soon as he did that, I could hear dogs barking.

"This is probably the time of day he feeds the dogs," Tom said.

In a little while Mr. Bartell came out of the barn with a bucket. He went to the hand pump for the well and pumped a bucket full of water. He took it into the barn.

"I was right," Tom said. "He's feeding and watering the dogs."

"Is that what we came here to find out?" I asked.

"One of the reasons," Tom said. "I want to know what he does next."

Mr. Bartell got a second bucket of water from the well. He went into the barn. When he came out again, he locked the padlock. Then he watered the team of horses. After that he went inside the farmhouse for a long time. When he came out, he began walking toward town.

Tom and I ran back to our bikes the way we'd come. We could see Mr. Bartell from the apple orchard as he started down Main Street. "You take the bicycles home," Tom said, "so I can follow him on foot, hiding behind trees. I don't want him to find out he's being watched."

Tom arrived home as I was washing my hands for lunch.

"Mr. Bartell went to the Palace Cafe," Tom told me. "I got Basil to watch him there for me."

When we'd finished our lunch, Tom and I went to the alley behind the cafe. Tom knocked on the kitchen door. Basil opened the door a crack to see who it was, then came out.

"Where did Mr. Bartell go after he ate?" Tom asked.

"To the Fairplay Saloon," said Basil.

Tom looked at me. "There's nothing for Mr. Bartell to do at the farm," he said. "I'll bet he spends all afternoon in the saloon."

Basil nodded. "That's what Mr. Bartell usually does," he said. "Then he comes here to eat his supper."

"Let's go, J.D.," Tom said.

We rode our bicycles to the meat market.

"Why are we stopping here?" I asked.

"To get meat scraps," Tom answered.

We had to wait for Mr. Thompson to finish taking care of a customer.

"Your mother didn't phone in an order," he told us.

"We aren't here because of that," Tom said. "What do you do with your meat scraps?"

"Either give them to someone who wants them or throw them away at the end of the day," Mr. Thompson said. "That fellow Bartell came around wanting me to save meat scraps for him. I told him I don't hold with dogfighting, and if he wants meat for his animals, he'll have to buy it. I do sell horse meat for dogs."

"Will you please give us the meat scraps every day?" Tom asked. "We'll come for them right after lunch."

"Sure thing." Mr. Thompson looked behind his counter. "Do you want what I have on hand now?"

"Yes, please," Tom said.

Mr. Thompson got a piece of wrapping paper. He dumped the meat scraps from a box onto the paper. He rolled up the meat scraps and handed them to Tom.

"Thank you very much," Tom said.

We left the meat market and went home. Tom got a hammer from the toolshed. Then we rode back out to the Kingston farm.

We hid our bicycles in the long weeds so anyone passing on the road couldn't see them, and walked to the rear of the barn. Tom pried a board loose with the hammer. Then he nailed it so it would swing back and forth. We entered the barn.

There was enough light coming through the cracks to see pretty well. The first thing I noticed was the six cages along one side of the barn. Each cage held a barking dog.

"That's the pit," Tom said, pointing.

We walked over to look at it. The pit was about ten feet wide and twelve feet long. The boards around it were about four feet high. There was a sliding door on one side of the pit.

"That's where Mr. Bartell must put the dogs before the fight," Tom said.

I turned away from the pit and went to look at the dogs. One of them, a bulldog, had scars all over his face and body. There was a sign on his cage reading KILLER MCCOY. In the next cage was a dog that kept barking at us and showing his teeth. His name was Blue Devil. The other four looked like regular dogs, except they were barking and baring their teeth at us.

"They sure look vicious," I said.

Tom walked to the front of Killer McCoy's cage. He held his hand close to the bars for the dog to smell. "That's a good boy," he said. Then he fed Killer some meat scraps through the bars.

Tom continued down the line of cages, letting each dog smell his hand to get his scent, then feeding it some of the meat scraps. When the meat was gone, Tom went to each cage and spoke to the dogs.

"That's a good boy," he told each dog.

A couple of the dogs still growled at Tom, but the others stopped barking and began to whine. All of them, even the dogs who growled, slowly wagged their tails as if they didn't know what to think. As we left the barn, they began barking again.

"What is your great brain's plan?" I asked as we rode our bikes back to town.

"You'll see," Tom said. "If it works."

The next day Basil called right after we'd finished lunch. He told Tom over the telephone that Mr. Bartell had eaten lunch in the cafe and then went to the Fairplay Saloon.

Tom and I immediately went to the meat market, where we picked up the meat scraps Mr. Thompson had saved for us. Then we rode our bikes out to the Kingston farm. We entered the barn through the board Tom had loosened.

The dogs began barking as soon as they saw us, but they didn't sound as vicious as they had the day before.

Tom spoke to each dog and fed it a scrap of meat. Then he went to Killer McCoy's cage. He talked to the dog for a while and fed it some more meat. By then Killer was wagging his tail.

Still talking, Tom slowly unhooked the door. He patted the dog on the head and fed him another scrap of meat. Then he let Killer out of his cage.

Although the dog no longer seemed dangerous, I became frightened. "What if we can't get him back in the cage?" I asked.

"Stop worrying," Tom said. "Let me and my great brain handle this."

Tom played gently with Killer for a few minutes. Then he walked over to Blue Devil's cage.

I could see how that dog got its name. Its fur was almost blue in color. It was some kind of hound dog, with one ear completely chewed off. There were scars on its shoulders from dogfights.

Tom spoke softly to Blue Devil, who looked at Tom and wagged his tail. Then Blue Devil saw Killer McCoy and bared his teeth.

"Good boy," Tom said, giving each dog some food.

By that time Killer must have been pretty full, but he ate anyway. Blue Devil wolfed his scrap down and whined for more. Tom very slowly unhooked the cage door and opened it.

Killer began to growl, and both dogs showed their teeth.

"Stop that," Tom said. "You fellows are going to be friends."

He fed each dog another scrap of meat. Then he walked to the end of the barn with both dogs following him. He laid down the paper with the rest of the scraps. After the dogs finished eating, he petted each one on the head and talked to them.

Blue Devil began running around the inside of the barn and barking as if he were enjoying his freedom. Killer watched for a moment, and then he began running too.

Tom let the dogs have fun for a few minutes. Then he grabbed Blue Devil by the fur of the neck and led the dog back to his cage. After that he locked up Killer.

Before we left, Tom went by each cage, speaking to each dog and telling them they were good dogs. "That's it for today," he told me.

The next afternoon we again went to the Kingston farm. Tom fed Killer and Blue Devil some meat scraps, then let them out of their cages. The dogs began chasing each other as if they were old friends.

While Killer and Blue Devil played, Tom fed and talked to the other dogs. A dog by the name of Hornet had been watching Killer and Blue Devil play. He scratched at his door and whined to be let out of his cage.

When Tom finally opened Hornet's cage door, the dog made tracks straight to where Blue Devil and Killer were playing. In no time at all, there were three dogs chasing one another around the barn.

By the end of the week, we were letting all the dogs out of their cages every afternoon to run. They would play tag around the barn floor and through the bales of hay, but there was not one fight among them.

The dogs all seemed to be friends now, but Tom wanted to make sure. The afternoon before the day of the dogfights, he put Killer into the pit by himself. Then he put Blue Devil into the space behind the sliding door. He waited until he figured each dog knew where the other was, then slowly slid the door open.

Blue Devil walked into the pit, looking as if he wasn't certain what to do. When Killer came toward him, he growled and bared his teeth. Killer growled right back.

"Easy," Tom said. "Good dog."

Killer and Blue Devil each thought Tom was speaking to him. They both stopped growling and looked up at Tom.

"Good dog," Tom repeated. Then he climbed down into the pit with them.

I'll tell you, I held my breath, but Tom knew what he was up to. The dogs came up to him, then sniffed each other peacefully.

"J.D.," Tom said. "Get Hornet and put him in the pit."

It wasn't long until all six dogs were playing in the pit together. The only problem we had was that a couple were having such a good time they didn't want to go back to their cages. But of course The Great Brain had already prepared for that eventuality. He put some meat scraps in the cages and the dogs went in to eat.

The Saturday of the dogfights, Tom and I ate an early lunch. Then we once again stopped for meat scraps and rode out to the Kingston farm. We hid our bicycles in the orchard and sneaked through the weeds to the ridge.

We waited until Mr. Bartell came out of the farmhouse and went to the barn. Then we hightailed it to the rear of the barn where the loose board was located.

I could see Mr. Bartell through a crack between the boards. He had a bullwhip and was going from cage to cage, beating on the cages with the whip.

"What is he doing that for?" I whispered.

"To get the dogs excited," Tom whispered back. "I'd bet he didn't feed them either, to make them nervous."

The dogs were nervous and excited all right. They were barking and snarling like crazy.

Mr. Bartell gave the dogs some water, then left the barn.

"Let's go," Tom said as he moved the board aside.

"Where?" I asked.

"Inside the barn and up in the hayloft," Tom said. "We can't see from here."

I followed Tom into the barn. When the dogs smelled him, they quieted down and only barked as if in greeting.

After Tom fed and talked to each dog, we climbed a ladder to the hayloft. There was very little hay in the loft.

Tom lay down on the floor and tried looking through several cracks before he motioned for me to lie down beside him. By looking through the crack, I could see the pit and all around it.

We lay there for what seemed like hours before Mr. Bartell returned to the barn and stationed himself near the door. Very soon the customers began to arrive. After Mr. Bartell had collected a dollar from each one, they walked around, looking at the pit and eyeing the dogs.

"The fight will be between Killer McCoy and Blue Devil," Mr. Bartell told them, "in case you men want to bet."

Right away several of the customers made bets with one another.

When there were about fifty men in the barn, Mr. Bartell closed the door. The men crowded around the pit, laughing and talking and still placing bets.

Mr. Bartell got Killer out of his cage and pushed the dog through the sliding door into the pit. Then he took Blue Devil and put him into the place behind the sliding door.

"Last chance to bet!" Mr. Bartell yelled. Then he shoved the sliding door open.

As he did that, noise filled the barn. Men shouted at one another and at the dogs. Those dogs still in their cages barked louder. Beside me in the loft, Tom changed position to look through a different crack.

Blue Devil ran out from behind the door into the pit. He spotted Killer, and the two dogs just looked at each other. Then Killer sat down.

"Fight, you worthless bags of bones!" Mr. Bartell shouted.

When neither dog moved, Mr. Bartell picked up his bullwhip and began to beat them.

73

All Killer and Blue Devil did was whine and run from one end of the pit to the other, trying to get away from the whip.

"Fake!" a cowboy yelled.

Then everybody took up the cry, "Fake!"

Mr. Bartell put up his hands. "Hold on a minute!" he shouted. "There are times a dog just doesn't feel like fighting. I'll get two of my other dogs."

Mr. Bartell put Killer and Blue Devil back in their cages. Then he put Hornet and another dog into the pit together.

Hornet and the other dog sniffed at each other. Then, I'll be darned if those two dogs didn't start playing together, not fighting at all, but sort of wrestling and playing chase.

"Some dogfight!" somebody yelled.

"I don't know what's gotten into these dogs," Mr. Bartell said. "They are trained to fight immediately. Let me try my other two dogs."

But the last two dogs wouldn't fight either, not even when Mr. Bartell went after them with his whip.

"Sic 'em," he yelled, lashing out at them.

I closed my eyes tightly as the whip came down across the dogs' backs. Then I eased them open again.

One of the cowboys had grabbed the bullwhip from Mr. Bartell. "You and your phony dogfights!" he shouted. "I ought to take this whip to you."

"I want my money back!" somebody yelled.

The way the men crowded around Mr. Bartell, I thought they were going to use the whip on him for sure.

Mr. Bartell must have thought so too. "You can have your money!" he said, sounding scared. "No hard feelings!"

A man with a black beard answered, "For you, maybe. We ought to string you up from one of those rafters." Then

74

he began tearing boards off the side of the pit, and several men joined him until the pit had been completely destroyed.

The cowboy who'd grabbed the whip from Mr. Bartell got his dollar back, then opened the sliding door and whistled to the dogs still in the pit.

They came running out and headed straight for the barn door. A man near the door opened it, and the dogs ran right outside.

"Turn the rest of them loose!" the man with the black beard yelled. He grabbed Mr. Bartell by the collar.

"We don't take kindly to your type around here," he said. "You have fifteen minutes to hitch up your team and clear the area. You take longer, and we'll tar and feather you and ride you out of town on a rail."

It didn't take Mr. Bartell fifteen minutes. He must have been gone in less than ten.

As for the dogs, four of them were later picked up by ranchers for pets or watchdogs. But two of them, Killer McCoy and Blue Devil, were never seen again.

To this very day, I don't know what happened to those two dogs, but that Saturday afternoon in the Kingston barn I knew one thing for certain. The Great Brain had done it again.

CHAPTER SIX

Smoke

THE MONDAY AFTER Tom put an end to the Adenville dogfights, Papa received an order to print a large number of pamphlets for the Mormons. So Papa put Tom back to work, and I hardly saw my brother at all for the next few weeks.

It was while I was with the other fellows that I first saw a boy my age smoke. That boy was Parley Benson. Parley had been talking about smoking for quite a while, but nobody paid any attention to him until that day.

We'd all gone down to the swimming hole that afternoon. Most of us had our clothes off and were ready to go into the river when Parley stopped us.

"I'm going to smoke a cigarette," he said.

Danny Forester wasn't working that afternoon, so he was going swimming with us. His left eyelid flipped wide open, then went half closed again.

"You got tobacco and everything?" he asked.

"Who needs tobacco?" Parley said. He went and got some dried bark from a tree. He crushed it and rolled it in the palms of his hands. Then he took a piece of toilet paper from his pants pocket and put the bark in it. After a couple of tries, Parley had rolled a cigarette. He lit it with a match and then blew smoke out of his mouth.

"Now watch this," he said.

And I'll be a frog who can't croak if Parley didn't blow smoke out of his nose. It made him cough and sort of sneeze, but he did it.

"I'll pass it around," he said as he handed the cigarette to Danny Forester.

Danny took a puff and must have inhaled the smoke, because he began coughing like the devil and handed the cigarette to Herbie Sties.

Herbie took a puff of smoke, held it, and let it out slowly. There was a very strange look on his face as he offered the cigarette to Seth Smith. Seth shook his head, and so did the rest of us. Herbie handed the cigarette back to Parley.

Parley took a few more puffs, blowing the smoke through his nose, and then put the cigarette out in the sand. "You have to get used to it," he told Danny and Herbie.

"Not me," Danny said.

Herbie shook his head.

"Afraid to smoke a little cigarette," Parley teased.

"All it did was make me cough," Danny answered.

Parley looked at Herbie.

77

"It made me dizzy,

It made me sick,

I prefer sodas

Or ice cream to lick," Herbie said.

"Why do you want to smoke anyway?" Jimmie Peterson asked.

"Because it makes you a man," Parley said.

Danny coughed again. "Cigarettes can't make you five or six years older," he said.

"You fellows are just jealous," Parley said.

But I noticed Parley was a little pale, and he didn't do much swimming that afternoon. Most of the time he sat on the riverbank.

Since Tom was putting in full days at the *Advocate*, I didn't get a chance to tell him what had happened until he and Papa came home for supper. We were sitting on the back porch steps with Frankie, waiting for Mamma to call us to come to the table.

"Parley smoked a cigarette at the swimming hole today," I said. "Danny and Herbie took a puff, but nobody else did."

"Where'd he get the tobacco?" Tom asked. "His father doesn't smoke, just chews."

"He used bark from a tree," I told him.

"The Indians always mix the bark of willow trees with their tobacco," Tom said.

"Parley just smoked the plain old bark," I said.

"Know something, J.D.?" Tom said. "My great brain has to know everything, and I've noticed that almost every man in town who isn't a Mormon smokes or chews tobacco. The Mormons can't smoke because it's against their religion, but practically all the Gentiles do. Papa smokes his pipe and cigars. There must be a good reason why so many men smoke. My great brain will never be satisfied until I find out that reason."

I didn't learn what Tom had in mind until the following Sunday after dinner, which we ate at one o'clock as usual. Tom told me to come with him to the barn. We went up the rope ladder to his loft, then pulled the ladder up after us so Frankie couldn't come too.

Tom took a Bull Durham sack from his pocket.

"Where'd you get that?" I asked, because it was against the law to sell tobacco to anybody under the age of eighteen.

"I picked the sack up in the street," Tom said. "I put some of Papa's pipe tobacco in it."

From another pocket, Tom took some toilet paper. It took him three tries before he managed to roll a cigarette.

Tom's cigarette didn't look as good as Parley's had. It was fat in the middle and small at both ends.

Tom lit the cigarette and took several puffs.

"What's it like?" I asked.

Tom made a face. "Pretty awful," he said. "I guess a fellow has to practice to build up tolerance."

"Maybe men smoke to prove they can withstand torture," I said.

"I don't think so." Tom took a couple more puffs and then threw the cigarette in a bucket of water he kept in the loft in case of fire. "Don't worry, my great brain will figure out the reason."

"While you're thinking about it, want to come along to Smith's vacant lot?" I asked. "All the fellows will be there."

"Thanks, J.D.," Tom said, "but I guess I'll stroll on over to see Polly."

I thought maybe Tom would forget all about smoking, but he was right when he said his great brain would never be satisfied until it discovered why men smoke. Every evening that week before he went to see Polly, he went up in his loft and smoked a cigarette. I went along and watched.

Friday I forgot to pull the rope ladder up after me. Tom had just taken out his tobacco and papers when Frankie's head and shoulders came above the loft. Frankie remained standing on the ladder.

"Whatcha doing?" he asked.

"Beat it," Tom said.

"You're making a cigarette," Frankie said. "That's wrong."

"I'm only trying an experiment," Tom said. "Now go away."

Frankie went back down the ladder. Tom finished making his cigarette, lit it, and blew smoke through his mouth.

"Smoking will stunt your growth," I said. "You'll stop growing if you smoke."

"That's silly," Tom said.

"Did your great brain find out why men smoke?" I asked.

Tom took another puff on his cigarette, blew the smoke out slowly, and looked at the barn beams far over our heads. "I have an idea," he said. "I'll tell you when I know for certain."

"Bet you can't blow smoke through your nose," I said, "like Parley did."

"There's nothing to it." Tom took a puff and blew smoke from his nose just as Papa came up the rope ladder and stopped with his head and shoulders above the loft.

80

"Put out that cigarette and come with me," Papa ordered.

Tom threw the cigarette in the bucket of water. We followed Papa down the rope ladder to the barn floor. Frankie was standing there.

"Tattletale," Tom said to him.

"Frankie did the right thing in telling me," Papa said. "Now, you come along."

We followed Papa into the kitchen, where he stopped. Aunt Bertha and Mamma were washing the dinner dishes.

"I want you both to see this," Papa said. "Let the dishes go and come into the parlor."

Mamma and Aunt Bertha dried their hands and followed us into the parlor. Papa sat down in his rocking chair. Mamma and Aunt Bertha sat in their chairs. Mamma folded her hands on her lap.

"I caught Tom smoking in the barn," Papa said. Then he looked at my brother. "I'm not going to permit you to sneak out to the barn to smoke. If you want to smoke, you will do it right here in the house. You may not smoke cigarettes, because they are bad for you, but you are permitted to smoke a pipe or cigar in the house anytime you want."

Mamma frowned. "Do you know what you are saying?" she demanded.

"I know perfectly well what I'm saying and doing," Papa said. "If our son is going to smoke, he is going to do it right here in this parlor."

Then he opened his humidor and removed two cigars. He cut off the ends with his cigar knife so they would draw. He handed one to Tom, then struck a match.

"Smoke to your heart's content," he said as he held the match to light Tom's cigar and then his own.

Tom sat down in a chair and took a puff on the cigar.

Frankie looked at him. "Bet you can't blow smoke rings like Papa," he said.

Tom got a mouthful of smoke and then tapped a finger on his cheek as he pursed his lips. He wasn't very good at it, but he managed to blow a couple of smoke rings.

"I declare," Mamma said. "Two cigars going at the same time in our parlor is too much for me. Come on, Bertha, let's finish those dishes."

After Mamma and Aunt Bertha left the room, Papa smiled at Tom. "Well, Son," he said, "how do you like it? There is nothing like a good cigar."

Tom gave Frankie and me a superior look as he puffed on the cigar. Then he must have inhaled some smoke, because he began to cough.

"Don't let that bother you," Papa said. "You'll get the hang of it in a little while."

For my money, it didn't look as if Tom was enjoying his cigar. His face was turning pale. Then, I'll be a cat with a dog's head if he didn't actually begin to turn green. He jumped up and put the cigar in an ashtray, then cupped his hand over his mouth and ran out of the parlor. I ran after him.

Tom went to the toilet and began to throw up. He kept throwing up until his stomach was empty. Then he staggered from the bathroom. His face was greenish white and his eyes were bleary.

Boy, oh, boy, did Tom look sick. Suddenly he turned and ran back into the bathroom. I could hear him heaving, but nothing came up. He came wobbling out into the hall again.

"Help me up the stairs, J.D.," he said in a weak voice.

I half carried him up to our bedroom. He flopped on

the bed and began groaning. I became so worried, I ran back down to the parlor.

"Tom's dying!" I cried.

"Far from it," Papa said, "but he is going to be a very sick boy for a while."

Mamma came from the kitchen and stood drying her hands on the skirt of her apron. "Wasn't that rather a mean trick to pull on your own son?" she asked.

"The results will justify the method," Papa said. "Would you rather have him sneaking cigarettes in the barn?"

"Of course not," Mamma said. "I just hate to see him so sick."

"The sicker he is, the more he'll hate the smell of tobacco," Papa said.

I ran back upstairs. Tom lay on his back and was groaning as if he were dying for sure. He was clutching the bedspread.

"The room is spinning around and the bed is tipping over," he cried.

"No, it isn't," I told him.

"It sure feels like it," Tom said.

"Maybe you'd better get undressed and stay in bed," I said.

"I'm too sick to get undressed," Tom said. "Stand still, J.D. Stop spinning around."

"You only imagine that because your great brain is bamboozled by the tobacco," I said. "Come on, I'll help you get undressed."

It was a struggle, but I finally got Tom undressed and into bed. He kept grabbing at the bedclothes or putting his hands against the wall.

"The room won't stop spinning," he complained.

"Shut your eyes," I said.

Tom shut his eyes but opened them almost immediately. "That only makes it worse," he told me.

Mamma had come to stand in the doorway. "You'll feel better by morning," she said. "J.D., you'd better run over to the Reagans' and tell Polly that Tom can't visit her this evening."

By the next morning, Tom was well enough to get up. He was hungry too. He ate a big bowl of cornmeal mush and some soft-boiled eggs for breakfast.

When Papa finished his eggs and toast, he stood and stretched. Then he took his big watch from its pocket and looked at it. "I have time for a cigar before I go to work," he said to Tom. "Would you care to join me?"

"I'm never going to smoke again," Tom said. "I'll just go along with J.D. while he does his chores."

Tom and I walked out to the barn where I fed and watered our livestock. While I was fetching water for the team of horses, Tom asked, "Did you tell Polly I was dying?"

"I told her you smoked a cigar and were as sick as all get out from it."

"What did she say?" Although Tom was much better, his skin was still pale. His freckles seemed larger and more orange than normal.

"She said she hates the way cigars smell, and cigarettes too."

Tom nodded. "That proves it," he told me.

"Proves what?"

"What my great brain figured out was the reason men smoke."

I poured one bucket of water into the horses' trough, then the second. "Why?" I asked as I headed back to the pump for more water.

"Because women don't like it."

I stopped walking so suddenly that one of the buckets banged into my leg. "I don't think so," I told him, "or Mamma and Papa would never have gotten married."

"Why, J.D.," Tom said, his voice sounding irritated, "haven't you noticed how women smell different from men?"

"Mamma smells of soap and baking and sachet," I pointed out.

"And Papa?"

"Of printer's ink and cigar smoke."

"Which smell do you like best?" Tom asked.

"Mamma's, of course," I told him.

"Now, let me explain to you," Tom said. "When a fellow smokes, he stinks like tobacco, making him less attractive to women. That makes women a lot less interested in that fellow. Also, smoking cancels out a lot of a man's sense of smell. Therefore, the man who smokes can't smell a woman's sachet or soap and such."

"You wanted to break Polly's spell on you," I said hopefully.

"Of course not! You must have too much wax in your ears. You didn't hear a thing I've been saying."

"I did too. I can't help it if I have a little brain."

"What I mean is that it's *harder* for a girl to put a spell on a fellow if he smokes," Tom said. He spoke slowly and distinctly, as if my brain was less than donkey sized.

"Oh, I see. If Papa didn't smoke, Mamma could make him do anything she wanted him to."

"Right," Tom said.

"Boy, oh, boy, do I feel sorry for you," I said.

"Why?"

"Because you are under Polly's spell forever, either that or deadly sick every night."

"I wish it weren't so hard to explain things to you, J.D.," Tom said. "I am not under a spell, and even if I were, it wouldn't matter, because in a few weeks I am leaving for Boylestown, Pennsylvania, to go to high school."

"Don't they have any girls in Boylestown?" I asked, thinking that if that were so, I could hardly wait to go there.

"There are girls, but not at the school. And Sweyn told me that the boys at the school are not permitted to walk out with girls."

That was when Papa shouted to Tom to get a move on. Tom went off to work at the *Advocate* and I went back to my chores. But the whole time I was watering and feeding our cow, I was thinking about what Tom's great brain had figured out about men and smoking. The more I thought about it, the more sense it made. The only thing I couldn't understand was why Parley had to smoke. Parley goes so long between baths that no girl with a nose in working condition would ever want to put a spell on him.

When I finished my morning chores, I went to the parlor. It was quiet and sort of dark because Mamma closes the draperies during the day to keep the sunlight from fading the rug. I went to Papa's humidor, picked a cigar from it, and took the cigar up to my room.

I sat on my bed for a while, looking at the cigar. It didn't smell too awful since it wasn't lit, and it didn't look all that dangerous either. Still, I had seen with my very own eyes how sick it could make a fellow.

I only had a little brain, but there was one thing I did

know. Tom had a great brain, and Polly still was able to put a spell on him. I rubbed the cigar behind my ears and on my cheeks and wrists, where I'd seen Mamma put sachet powder. Then I hid the cigar under my mattress where I could get to it every morning without Tom or anyone else seeing me.

Tom and his great brain had figured out the reason men smoke. Me and my little brain had figured out that I was getting closer to age thirteen all the time and that any day a girl might try to put a spell on me.

I was not taking any chances.

CHAPTER SEVEN

Blue Lake

I FIGURED I WOULD NOT need my cigar for protection against girls on our annual summer camping and fishing trip. We boys always looked forward to this trip. It meant ten days of glorious fishing, hunting, and exploring. We liked being alone with Papa too, away from civilization and his work at the *Advocate*. So we were all disappointed one evening during a supper of hickory-smoked ham and homemade baked beans when Papa announced he couldn't go this summer.

"I want to attend the newspaper publishers' convention in Denver," he said.

Tom swallowed a mouthful of food. "Why can't you do both?" he asked.

"People are used to missing one edition of the *Advocate* each year," Papa said. "They know a newspaper publisher is entitled to a vacation. But to do both I'd have to miss two and possibly three editions. However, there is nothing to prevent you boys from going without me."

Mamma shook her head. "I will not permit the boys to go alone," she said.

"Why not?" Papa asked. "They are old enough to take care of themselves."

"Sweyn D. and Tom D. might be," Mamma said, "but not John D. and Frankie."

I didn't like being told I was a baby. "I'm plenty old enough to take care of myself," I said.

Frankie nodded. "Me too," he said.

"I think they'll be all right," Papa said. "They can go to Beaver Canyon. There are always adults fishing there this time of year."

"Sweyn D. has to work at the hospital," Mamma said, "and the others are too young to go without him."

"Dr. LeRoy told me I could have a week off anytime I wanted as a vacation," Sweyn told her, "so there is no problem."

Mamma hemmed and hawed for a while, but she finally agreed that we could go as long as we didn't stay longer than a week. "And, remember," she said, "I'm counting on all of you to watch each other, and especially to look out for Frankie."

Three days later we left home early in the morning.

Tom was driving our team. Frankie and I sat on the seat of the buckboard beside him. Sweyn was riding his mustang, Dusty.

At noon we stopped by a dried-up streambed and ate our lunch. Mamma had prepared a big meal of fried chicken, hard-boiled eggs, and bread-and-butter sandwiches for us, every bite delicious. Right then I began worrying. On our previous fishing and camping trips, Papa had always been the cook.

"What are we going to do without Papa to do the cooking?" I asked.

Tom looked as if he were disgusted with me for asking such a dumb question. "I'll do the cooking," he said. "I've watched Papa plenty of times and can cook as good as he can."

When we arrived at Beaver Canyon that afternoon, there were a lot of people fishing along the banks and out in the water. Instead of pulling in beside the other wagons, Tom kept going. Sweyn rode up beside us.

"How about making camp?" he asked.

"Why stop here?" Tom said. "Let's go lake fishing on top of the mountain."

"I know there are lakes on top of the mountain, but how do you know where they are?" Sweyn asked.

"People haul ice from the lakes during the winter," Tom said. "All we have to do is follow their road until we come to a lake."

"But we don't have a boat," Sweyn protested.

"Lake trout feed near the banks," Tom said. "Don't worry. We'll catch plenty of fish."

We arrived on top of the mountain in the late afternoon.

91

There was a road all right, but it was overgrown because it hadn't been traveled since winter.

Sweyn rode up beside us. "The lake could be a good distance away," he said. "Maybe we should make camp here."

"It can't be far," Tom said. "I believe this is the way to Blue Lake."

After we'd ridden another hour, Tom pulled up the team. "Look at those trees," he said, pointing. "The lake must be over there."

Tom was right. We arrived at Blue Lake at sunset. We hobbled the horses and turned them loose to graze and drink from the lake. Then we pitched our tent. We built a camp fire; then Tom heated four cans of pork and beans in a frying pan.

"Too late to make biscuits," he said. "We'll eat canned goods now and fish for breakfast."

Frankie shook his head stubbornly. "I want sourdough biscuits now," he said.

"Well, you're not going to get them," Tom said.

It began to get cold after we ate. I was glad Mamma had insisted we take plenty of blankets. We wrapped ourselves up in them and sat around the camp fire.

"We'll hit the hay early," Tom said, "and get up early to catch fish for breakfast."

I had a hard time going to sleep that night. I could hear the wind rustling in the trees and coyotes and wolves howling. The ground seemed hard after my nice feather mattress at home. But finally I fell asleep.

When I woke up, Tom and Sweyn were gone. I woke Frankie and we dressed, then went outside the tent. I could see Tom and Sweyn fishing along the banks of the lake.

Blue Lake's water was as blue as the sky overhead. It was a big lake too. I judged it about a half-mile wide and a mile long. I got my fishing pole, and Frankie got his. We walked down to where Tom was.

As we arrived, Tom landed a beauty of a lake trout. He removed the hook, then took the tree branch he'd trimmed into a Y shape from the lake water. He added the trout he'd just caught to the four fish already strung onto the stick.

"Hey, S.D.," he shouted. "How many fish have you caught?"

"Four nice big ones," Sweyn hollered back.

"That's plenty," Tom shouted. "Let's go have some breakfast."

Sweyn cleaned the fish while Tom kneaded sourdough. The dough got its name from the fermented dough prospectors carried to use as a leaven in biscuits. Because of this, prospectors were often called sourdoughs.

After Tom shaped the dough, he put the biscuits into our Dutch oven to cook. He greased a big frying pan with bacon, then rolled four trout in flour and put them on to fry. Sweyn fixed the coffee.

While we ate fried fish and biscuits, Tom fried up some potatoes, then the rest of the fish. We must have been hungry, because we ate everything, even all the sourdough biscuits. Afterward, Frankie and I washed our tin plates, cups, knives, and forks in the lake.

Sweyn got the shotgun from the tent. "I'm not going to eat fish for five days," he told us. "I'll see if I can get us some rabbits for lunch."

Frankie and I stayed at the camp, fishing along the banks with Tom. Blue Lake was plumb full of trout. I could see

93

them jumping to catch insects. In no time at all we had caught more than we needed. Tom put them on his Y stick and left them in the water.

During the time we were fishing, I heard Sweyn fire the shotgun three times. When the sun was almost directly overhead, he came down from the mountain. He was holding two rabbits.

"I missed one," he said, "but two are enough. I'll clean them."

We had fried rabbit and potatoes for lunch, then washed the dishes and went exploring around the lake. There were plenty of squirrels in the trees, but we didn't shoot any, as none of us cared for squirrel meat. There were plenty of birds, mostly jays that perched in the cedar trees. Then we returned to camp and went swimming until it was time to get supper.

"How about some trout and beans with sourdough biscuits?" Tom asked.

"Suits me," I told him.

"As long as there are biscuits," Frankie said.

"I'm hungry enough to eat the bean can," Sweyn said.

We were sitting around the camp fire after supper when three men rode into our camp leading a packhorse. They looked as if they had ridden a long way. The leader of the three was a big man with a red beard.

"Fix us some supper, boy," he told Sweyn when they'd dismounted.

"I'm not your boy," Sweyn said, "and I don't remember asking you to supper."

The big man walked over to Sweyn. He hit my brother hard along one side of his jaw. Sweyn went tumbling backward, then sat up, holding his face in both hands.

"That'll teach you not to talk back to Red Wade," he said.

"Leave him alone," Tom said. "I'll fix you some supper. Are bacon with beans and sourdough biscuits all right?"

"You got any spuds?" Red Wade asked.

"Yes," Tom said.

"Then fry some up," Red Wade said. "I fancy a mess of potatoes tonight, but I warn you. Tomorrow morning I want fish for breakfast. We ain't had nothing but beans to eat for two days."

While Tom was preparing the meal, Frankie walked over to Red Wade. "Are you men outlaws?" he asked.

"Whatever gave you that idea?" the big man said.

"Because you're mean," Frankie said. "You hit my brother."

"And that makes us outlaws." Red Wade laughed a sort of dirty laugh.

Tom looked up from the frying pan over the camp fire. "What are you doing in this part of the country?" he asked. "You don't have any fishing gear, so I know you didn't come up here to fish."

"Nosey kid, aren't you?" Wade said. "But just so you don't try anything foolish, I'll tell you we held up the mine payroll at Castle Rock. We had to kill a man to do it."

One of the outlaws, with such a thin face his cheekbones stuck out, spoke up. "Why are you telling these kids our business?"

"Simmer down, Bill," Wade said. "These kids aren't going anyplace and neither are we for a while. I reckon as how this is a good place to rest up our horses for a day."

The other outlaw had mean, squinty-looking eyes. He rolled a chew of tobacco into his jaw. "Gotta give you credit,

Red," he said. "Staying away from the road and going over the mountain was a good idea."

Wade grinned. "That posse is lookin' for us in the flatlands and desert. Fooled 'em completely, Jake."

"How long do you reckon it'll take us to get to Arizona?" Jake asked.

"Don't rightly know," Wade said. "I never been in this part of the country before. But if we keep heading south, we'll run into Arizona. We can pull a few jobs there to fatten our roll on the way to Mexico."

That was when I first started to feel frightened. The outlaws couldn't leave us if we knew where they were headed. I had a feeling in my bones that they were going to kill us.

Tom finished cooking the supper. We watched the outlaws eat it. Then we washed the dishes. When we went back to the camp fire, Wade was smoking a cigar.

"I told you if you stuck with me, you'd be in clover," he said to the other men. "Better than a thousand apiece in that mine payroll. A couple jobs in Arizona and we'll be on easy street when we hit Mexico."

Jake, who had the mean eyes, shook his head. "I don't like you talking so much in front of these kids," he said.

"I told you not to worry about them," Wade said. "You take first watch, Jake, until midnight. Bill, take the second, and I'll take the last. I know they are only kids, but they might try something foolish." He looked at Sweyn. "You kids better turn in now."

Sweyn didn't give him any back talk this time. He was still nursing his jaw and hadn't said a word after the outlaw hit him.

I had a hard time going to sleep that night, although Tom, Sweyn, and Frankie didn't. I couldn't understand how

Tom could sleep at all. With his great brain he must have known the outlaws would kill us. That way we couldn't tell the sheriff which way they had gone.

The next morning Sweyn had a big bruise covering the whole left side of his face. He didn't talk much and he hardly ate any breakfast. What he did eat, he chewed very slowly.

Between Tom, Sweyn, Frankie, and me, we had caught enough fish for all of us for breakfast. After eating, Red Wade rubbed his stomach.

"You kids put out good grub," he said. "What in the way of food do you have with you?"

"Bacon, potatoes, hard tack, cans of pork and beans, sourdough and flour, canned milk, and coffee," Sweyn said.

"We'll be taking that with us when we leave," Wade told us with a curt nod.

"It's enough to take you well into Arizona," Tom said. He took his compass from his pocket and looked at it. Then he pointed. "That second peak toward the right is due south."

"Gimme that." Wade grabbed the compass. "We might get a cloudy day and not have sun to guide us." He stuffed the compass into his pants pocket.

I had a hard time waiting until we were away from the outlaws so I could tell Tom my fears. "I know Red Wade plans to kill us," I said as we were washing the breakfast dishes. "Aren't you worried?"

"My great brain is working on it," was all he said.

That was the longest day of my life. We fished until we had plenty of fish for lunch. Then Jake took our shotgun and some shells. He went hunting and killed some rabbits. When he returned to camp, he gave the rabbits to Tom to prepare for supper.

While Sweyn helped Tom clean the rabbits, they talked

in low voices. It was clear that they were both worried, Sweyn worse than Tom. "I figure we have about twelve hours," he said. "We wouldn't be in this fix if we'd stayed in Beaver Canyon the way we were supposed to."

"My great brain got us into this, and my great brain will get us out," Tom said.

"I hope so," Sweyn answered. "I hate the thought of Mamma being told all her sons are goners at the same time."

When I thought of Mamma, my eyes started to get teary. I walked over to the camp fire, so I could pretend there was smoke in them.

The fried rabbit, potatoes, beans, and sourdough biscuits tasted good, but I wasn't hungry. I kept feeling that it was the last supper I'd ever eat. I didn't feel any better after the meal, when the outlaws discussed their plans.

Red Wade lit a cigar. "Reckon the horses are rested," he said. "We'll pull out first thing in the morning."

Jake squinted his mean little eyes at Sweyn, then Tom, then Frankie and me. "What about them kids?"

"No problem," Wade said. "I'll take care of it in the morning."

You can bet that I didn't get much sleep that night. I was certain as a racehorse can outrun a donkey that the outlaws would kill us in the morning. I could hear Frankie crying softly for a while, and then he must have fallen asleep. Sweyn tossed and turned for a long time, but Tom really surprised me. He went to sleep as if he were at home in his own bed.

I stayed awake, hoping that the outlaw left on guard would doze off. I had a crazy idea of somehow getting the shotgun and blasting them all to kingdom come. But it was just a crazy idea, because they all had guns and rifles as well as our shotgun.

It was just getting light when Wade ordered us all up.

"Fix us a breakfast of beans, potatoes, biscuits, bacon, and coffee," he ordered Tom.

Tom prepared the breakfast and we ate, although I mostly just pushed the food around with my fork. Then the outlaws took the rest of our food and loaded it onto their packhorse. I began to have some hope as they saddled up their horses, but not for long. They stood to one side, talking softly among themselves.

Then I heard Jake say, "We have to kill them. What difference does it make if we're wanted for one murder or for five?"

Tom, who'd been squatting on the ground near the camp fire, spoke up. "We are supposed to be home today," he said. He was lying, because we still had a few days left. "My uncle, Mark Trainor, is the marshal of Adenville and a deputy sheriff. When we don't arrive home, my mother will send him looking for us. He is the fastest gun in Utah. He killed the Laredo Kid and a dozen other outlaws. He will never stop looking for you until he's hunted you down and killed all of you."

"I've heard of your uncle," Red Wade said. "Reckon there is no need to kill you. If we tie you up, it'll take a couple of days for anyone to get up here and find you. That'll give us a good head start before Trainor can go back and get a posse."

He scratched at his chin beneath his whiskers. Then he said, "All right. Bill, you and Jake tie them up."

The two outlaws cut up Sweyn's lariat and tied us with

99

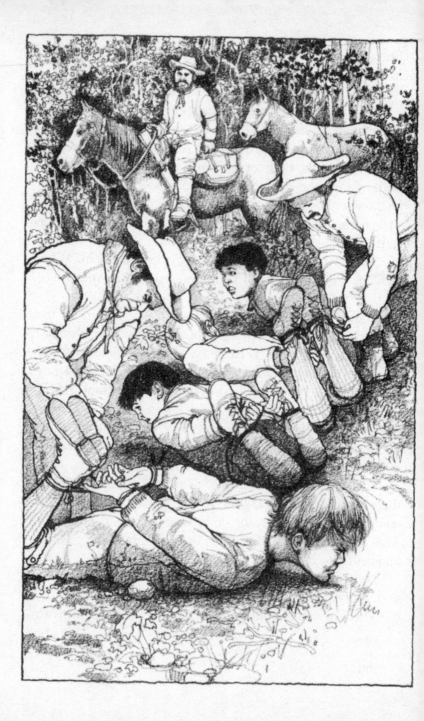

our hands and feet behind our backs. Jake pulled the knots awful tight on me. He really knew how to hog-tie a fellow.

"Just to make sure," Red Wade said, "we'll take your horses with us and turn them loose a few miles from here."

I was so scared, I couldn't even think until after the outlaws left leading our horses. Then I cried, "We're doomed! No one will look for us for days. The wolves and mountain lions will eat us."

"Stop with that doomed business," Tom ordered. "You're scaring Frankie."

"I suppose you aren't scared," I said.

"Scared of what?" he asked. "Now, shut up and do what I tell you. Roll over here by me."

It was awkward and difficult, but I managed to roll closer to Tom, wondering what he was going to do.

"Hold still," he said. "I'm going to try to untie you with my teeth."

Tom used his head and knees to get his head on my back. I could feel him nibbling at the lariat. He tried for quite a while and then gave up.

"Jake tied you too tight," he said. "Maybe Bill didn't tie Frankie so tight because he's little." Tom turned to Frankie, who was tied up next to him. "Lie still," he ordered.

Tom worked his head on top of Frankie's back. Then he began pulling at the knots with his teeth. He was at it so long I became worried.

"Too tight?" I asked.

Tom lifted his head to look at me. "I can get it if you just shut up and give me some time," he said.

Tom was right. He finally managed to loosen the knots on Frankie's wrists. Then Frankie untied his ankles himself.

All I can say is those outlaws really tied the knots on the

rest of us tight. Frankie wasn't able to undo them.

"Take my jackknife out of my pocket and cut the lariat," Tom told him.

In a few minutes we were all loose and rubbing our wrists.

"What now?" Sweyn asked, standing and stretching.

"We go get the horses," Tom said. "The outlaws think we're all tied up, so they won't risk slowing down to lead our horses more than a couple of miles." Tom looked at me. "J.D., you stay here with Frankie while S.D. and I track them down."

The outlaws had turned our team and Dusty loose just a few miles from camp. It wasn't long before Tom and Sweyn returned and hitched up the team. As we threw our gear into the back of the buckboard, I couldn't help thinking that Tom and his great brain had made one mistake.

"You shouldn't have let them know you had a compass," I told him.

"I wanted to be sure they headed due south," Tom said. "Now, get into the buckboard. We have some fast traveling to do."

"Why did you want them to head due south?" I asked as we headed back toward Beaver Canyon.

"You'll find out as soon as I see Uncle Mark and Sheriff Baker," Tom said, and that was all he would tell me.

We arrived in Adenville at dusk. Tom drove straight to the combination marshal's and sheriff's office. Both Uncle Mark and Sheriff Baker were there.

"I know the whereabouts of the men who robbed the payroll at Castle Rock and killed a man there," Tom said.

Both Uncle Mark and Sheriff Baker came out of their chairs. Sheriff Baker pulled at his walrus mustache. "They gave me and the posse the slip," he admitted.

"We left them at Blue Lake," Tom said. "They are Red Wade and two outlaws named Jake and Bill. They're riding right into a trap. None of them have ever been in this area of the country before, and they don't know the lay of the land."

Uncle Mark pushed his Stetson to the back of his head. "What trap?" he asked.

"They're headed for Arizona, due south from Blue Lake," Tom explained. "They have only about an eight-hour head start. They'll have to find a way to cross Bryce Canyon and the Grand Canyon, and that will slow them down."

Sheriff Baker spread a map on his desk. He ran his finger south from Blue Lake to Bryce Canyon and then on to the Grand Canyon.

"You're right," he said.

"Even if they find a crossing quickly at Bryce Canyon," Tom told him, "they'll end up at the Grand Canyon. Since they have to stay away from trails and roads, they will have a hard time finding a place to cross that."

Again Sheriff Baker traced the map with his finger. "They should come out of the mountains about here," he said. "By riding around the mountain on fast horses, we could cut them off." Then he stabbed his finger at a place near the rim of the Grand Canyon. "But we can make sure. This is the only place they can cross the Grand Canyon. We can beat them there. I'll get a posse together at once."

Tom was right about Bryce Canyon slowing down the outlaws. Sheriff Baker and the posse arrived at the crossing of the Grand Canyon several hours ahead of the outlaws. They set up a trap where they could catch Red Wade and his men in cross fire.

Although the outlaws didn't have a chance, they tried to shoot their way out. The outlaw named Jake was killed. Bill was wounded and died of his wounds before the posse could reach a doctor. Red Wade was also wounded, but lived to stand trial and was sentenced to be hanged.

Tom suffered one big disappointment. There was no state reward money for any of the outlaws, and the coal company must have figured that Sheriff Baker was just doing his job. Although they got the payroll money back, they didn't give a reward either.

The only reward Tom got was glory, but he made sure he received plenty of that. With Papa gone, Tom insisted he could get out a one-page extra of the *Advocate*. He wrote the story and set the type himself. I helped him run it off the press. LOCAL BOY HELPS CAPTURE WADE GANG read the headline.

When it came to writing the story, Tom had as much modesty as a plucked chicken hanging in a butcher-shop window. He did give credit to the posse for actually capturing Red Wade and killing the other two outlaws. But he let it be known that without the help of Thomas D. Fitzgerald this never would have happened.

As for me, I have no complaints. All I have to do is remember Red Wade and his squinty mean-eyed companion, Jake, and I get the shivers. Sweyn wasn't up to normal, Frankie was too young, and I know that my little brain never could have saved our skins. All our days left on earth we owe to Tom and his great brain.

CHAPTER EIGHT

The Swindler Is Swindled

EARLY ONE HOT and sunny morning in late August, two Paiute braves showed up in front of our house. One of the Indians was Running Bear, nephew of Chief Rising Sun. I'd never seen the other brave before. Both Indians were riding pinto horses, and each horse carried two large baskets filled with peaches.

Mamma, Frankie, Aunt Bertha, and I went out on the front porch to see what the Indians wanted.

Running Bear and the other brave swung down from their horses. Without saying a word or even seeming to notice us, they unloaded the baskets and put them on the porch.

The strange brave said something to Running Bear in Paiute. Running Bear grunted.

Then, holding his pinto by its bridle, Running Bear told Mamma, "The Great Chief Tav-Whad-Im send gift to white friend called Fitzgerald. Chief Tav-Whad-Im send greeting from all Paiute of Pa-Roos-Its band."

Before Mamma could so much as say "Thank you," Running Bear had mounted his horse. Giving a "Yip!" the braves rode off in a trail of dust.

"Land sakes!" Aunt Bertha said, placing one of her hands over her heart. "What will happen next?"

Mamma seemed not to hear Aunt Bertha. She was looking at the peaches. "What a fine gift," she said. "This should keep us in pies and preserves all winter."

"We'll have to get at them today," Aunt Bertha said, recovering enough to start checking the baskets. "These peaches are dead ripe."

My nose could tell me that. Already my mouth was watering from the thought of peach pie and from the delicious aroma of ripe peaches rising from the baskets.

"Can I have a peach?" Frankie asked, tugging at Mamma's apron.

Mamma smiled down at him. "Just one," she said, "but that's all for now. You'll want more later, and I don't want you to get a stomachache from too much fresh fruit."

"I won't," Frankie said, picking out a peach from the nearest basket.

"Rinse it off," Mamma said. "These peaches have probably traveled a long way, clear from Fruita, and there's bound to be trail dirt on them." Then she looked at Aunt Bertha.

"I'll check to make sure we have enough fruit jars," Mamma said, "and start heating up the range. Could you go over to the Z.C.M.I. store and get a twenty-five–pound sack of sugar?"

"As soon as I take off my apron and fix my hair," Aunt Bertha said, heading toward the door.

"Buy three dozen jar rings too," Mamma called after her. "Frankie, get your wagon. You and John D. haul these baskets to the backyard. After that, I want you to take your wagon along to the store to carry the sugar home. Remind Aunt Bertha to get some paraffin in case we decide to make jam."

"What should I do?" I asked, knowing there would be a lot of work that day.

"Fetch extra wood to the kitchen," Mamma told me. "Then set up the apple-butter kettle in the yard and lay a fire under it. We can scald the peaches out there and keep the kitchen range free for making syrup and for processing."

She headed into the house after Aunt Bertha, but turned back to say, "Don't go off after that, John D. I'll have plenty for you to do." Then she smiled and added, "Right now you can have a peach if you want one."

Did I ever! I picked the biggest, ripest peach I could find, and boy, oh, boy, was it good. That peach was so ripe the juice ran down the sides of my mouth and dripped off my chin.

It took me a while to get the apple-butter kettle set up and a fire laid under it. After that I had to fetch six buckets of water to fill the kettle. Just as I had a fire going, Frankie came running into the yard.

"Aunt Bertha fell!" he shouted. "She missed the step coming out of the Z.C.M.I. store and fell right on the sidewalk!"

"Did she get hurt?" I asked. If a fellow my age had fallen

over a measly step, he'd probably bounce, but Aunt Bertha was even older than Mamma and Papa, and she weighed a lot too.

"Only a little bit," Frankie said. "Dr. LeRoy says that her wrist is sprained and she must keep it in a sling for a week or so."

This was bad news. With a sprained wrist, Aunt Bertha couldn't possibly help with the heavy work of canning. She couldn't even peel the fruit or cut it up. I went into the kitchen to find out what Mamma was going to do.

"I feel plumb useless," Aunt Bertha was saying as Frankie and I came in the door.

"There's no use in crying over spilled milk," Mamma told her. "The truth of the matter is that I've gotten spoiled having you around to help me. And you can help some. If you aren't in too much pain, you can use your left hand to put the cut-up peaches in jars."

"It'll make me feel less useless," Aunt Bertha said.

Mamma looked at Frankie and me. "John D.," she said, "you go over to the *Advocate* and tell your father what happened. Ask him if he can spare Tom D. for the rest of the day. Frankie, you take chairs from the back porch to the yard and put them near the apple-butter kettle. You boys can peel and slice peaches on the grass instead of on the porch. That way the porch floor won't get all sticky from juice."

Luckily, Papa could spare Tom from the *Advocate*. "Tell your mother not to worry about the noon meal," he said to me. "I can eat over at the Palace Cafe."

Mamma looked a lot more cheerful when she saw Tom and heard what Papa had said. "Tell you what," she said. "Aunt Bertha and I were rolling out piecrusts when Running

Bear showed up. I'll turn some of the fruit into pies."

"That's a peach of an idea," Tom said, and then he laughed at his own joke.

Tom stopped laughing when he saw the four big baskets of fruit, the kettles, and the other equipment waiting. "That fruit will take all day to prepare," he said.

"Change your clothes first," Mamma told him. "I can handle everything inside, at least until the paring is done. You boys peel and halve the fruit. Tom D., you use the wire basket to scald the fruit. I don't want John D. to do that, as it's dangerous, and I don't want Frankie near the fire at all."

"All right," Tom said as he went off to change his clothes.

"Why do the peaches have to be scalded?" Frankie asked me as we waited for Tom to return.

"It makes them easier to peel," I said.

"What's in the kettles?" he asked, looking into the kettles we were to put our pared and cut-up peaches in.

"Just water with salt and vinegar in it," I told him. "The salt and vinegar keep the peaches from turning dark before Mamma puts them into fruit jars."

"I don't want to eat any peaches that are canned in salt and vinegar water," Frankie said.

I laughed. "Mamma drains it first," I explained. "Then after the peaches are in the jars, Mamma will pour hot sugar syrup over them. After that she puts them in the canner and boils them."

I sure was glad when Tom came back from changing his clothes and put an end to Frankie's questions. But I didn't like the expression in Tom's eyes. It meant his great brain was trying to come up with a plan to satisfy his money-loving heart.

So I was very suspicious when Tom said, "Frankie, run

109

over to Smith's vacant lot and tell the fellows they have an opportunity to earn some money. Tell them J.D. and I have a job for them."

"Oh, no," I said. "Include me out. You're going off to Boylestown in a few days, but I have to stay here in Adenville. I don't want my friends to think I'm a swindler."

Tom looked indignant. "Are you saying I would do something dishonest?" he asked.

"I'm not saying a word about you," I told him. "I'm only saying I don't want any part of it."

"All right, but you are passing up a great chance to invest some money and get out of work besides."

"That's okay by me." Every time I invested in one of Tom's deals, his pockets had ended up full of my money.

It wasn't long until Frankie was back. Parley Benson, Herbie Sties, and Jimmie Peterson were with him. Parley had on his usual beat-up clothes and coonskin cap. Herbie was wearing an old faded shirt and pants with patches on the knees and the seat.

Jimmie looked all dressed up by comparison with the other boys. He had his school pants and shirt on, since they were the only clothes that he could fit into.

"Frankie, run inside and get an old apron from Mamma for Jimmie," Tom said.

"I ain't wearing no apron!" Jimmie said.

"Then you're passing up a chance to earn ten cents, easy money," Tom said.

Now, ten cents was more money than many kids got their hands on in several weeks. Ten cents would buy two adventure magazines, or two large-size boxes of jujubes. It would buy a couple of sodas, or a good many other things at the Z.C.M.I. store. Ten cents wasn't anything to sneer at, so I wasn't surprised that Jimmie changed his mind. When Frankie handed him a faded old apron made of flour sacking, Jimmie put it on and sat in one of the chairs, prepared to work.

"I'll pay each of you fellows ten cents for helping peel and cut up these peaches," Tom said. "But you have to work hard, and you're not allowed to eat any."

When I heard Tom say that, I was glad I hadn't agreed to be in on his deal. His great brain must have been overworked at the *Advocate*, because it wasn't functioning right. Tom could get out of work by paying the fellows to do his share, but there was no way he could earn money.

By late morning I sure was glad that Tom had hired the other boys. My back was tired from bending over the pan I was cutting peaches into. My hands were wet and sore from peach juice, and every part of me felt sticky.

Tom sat in the shade of a nearby tree, watching the rest of us work. Every once in a while he'd take a peach from one of the baskets and eat it. The only other thing he did all morning was scald peaches and take pans of peaches into the house to Mamma.

We didn't see much of Mamma until she came out into the yard at about eleven o'clock.

"My," she said. "You boys certainly picked up some willing workers. It's all I can do to keep even with you."

"I can peel peaches
A whole big bunch.
What I'm wondering about is
Will I miss lunch," Herbie Sties said.

"I don't think so," Mamma answered, "not at the rate you are getting the peaches peeled. It will be a little late though. If I could, I'd fix you a meal, but I have too much work inside. How would you like some lemonade?"

"I'd like it just fine," Parley said. "I'm as thirsty as all get out."

"Me too," Jimmie agreed.

"I'll send some out in a few minutes," Mamma told us.

When Mamma said she'd send out the lemonade, I expected Aunt Bertha to bring it. I was really surprised when Polly Reagan came out of our kitchen door ten minutes later, carrying a tray holding a large pitcher of lemonade and six glasses.

When he saw her, Tom jumped up from where he was lounging under the tree and ran to take the tray from her hands.

I closed my eyes, plumb full of embarrassment. Then I cracked the lids and looked sideways at Jimmie, wondering if he'd noticed Tom had gone soft in the brain. But Jimmie was too busy trying to roll up his apron, as if to make it disappear.

As for me, I have to admit that a pitcher of lemonade makes a girl seem a lot more attractive. Maybe fancy food and drink is another way girls put spells on boys, I thought as I accepted a glass from Polly.

"I didn't know you were helping Mamma," Tom said, looking at the blue-and-white-striped apron Polly had on over her blue everyday dress.

"My mother was in the Z.C.M.I. store when your aunt Bertha fell on the step," Polly said. "She knew your mother would need extra help today, so she sent me on over." Then Polly frowned and looked at Tom.

"Aren't you working?" she asked.

"Oh, yes," Tom said. "I am scalding the peaches and

112

doing that kind of work. I'm paying Parley, Herbie, and Jimmie ten cents each to help too."

Tom had a prideful tone in his voice when he spoke of paying the other boys, as if he was somebody very important in Adenville, like the mayor.

Polly looked at him thoughtfully. "I'll have to tell my papa about that tonight," she said. "Papa always says, 'That Tom D. Fitzgerald could talk the buffalo down off a nickel.'"

"By jingo!" Parley shouted, and he began to laugh. The rest of the boys laughed too.

Tom managed to come up with a chuckle or two, but after Polly went back into the house, he was awful quiet. He didn't pick up a paring knife or anything, but he didn't look as if he were having as good a time lounging under the tree, not even with a glass of cool lemonade in his hand.

He did perk up about a half hour later when the smell of peach pie began to drift our way from the kitchen. He picked up his head, took a long sniff, rubbed his belly, and said, "Smell that, J.D. Mamma must be cooking the peach pies she promised me."

After Tom scalded the last of the peaches and gave them to us to peel and cut, he said, "I'll be back in a minute, fellows. I just want to check the progress of those pies."

"Bring your dimes with you," Parley said. "We're about done here."

When Tom returned, he had his dimes with him. "Here you are," he said, putting a dime into each boy's sticky palm. "Just as I promised. Ten cents for the morning's work. Nobody can ever say Tom D. swindled his friends."

We all knew that wasn't true, because in the past, before he was forced to reform, Tom D. had swindled every kid in town and a good number of adults too.

"It's too bad,
But I have a hunch
That for ten cents
I've missed my lunch," Herbie said sadly, eyeing the coin on his palm.

"Umm, smell those pies," Tom said. "Mamma made ten of them. She sent two home with Polly to thank her for her work, but the rest are mine."

"How do you figure that, T.D.?" I asked, thinking that Mamma had baked the pies for all of our family.

"Why, Chief Rising Sun sent those peaches to his friend, Fitzgerald," Tom said. "They must have been for me because I saved his nephew, Running Bear, from going to prison and also was responsible for freeing the two Paiute braves already there. So the peaches belong to me."

"Sure smell good," Parley said, tugging at his coonskin cap with one hand. Since his mother had died when Parley was very young, Parley probably hadn't tasted a fresh peach pie in years.

"I'll tell you what," Tom said. "I'll sell you a small piece of pie for five cents. If you want a big piece, say one-fourth of a pie, it'll be ten cents."

It didn't take Herbie two seconds to give up his dime. In another couple of seconds, Parley and Frankie handed over theirs.

"J.D.?" Tom said. "Frankie?"

"You didn't pay us for working," I told him.

"Way I figure it, you should pay me," Tom said. "If I hadn't hired Parley, Jimmie, and Herbie to help, you'd be knee-deep in peaches all afternoon."

I didn't answer, because what Tom said did make sense.

"You each give me ten cents," Tom said, "and I'll throw in a piece of pie for free."

"All right," I agreed.

"Frankie?"

"I guess so," Frankie said.

"J.D., come on in the house to get your and Frankie's money," Tom said. "Then you can help me carry out the pie for the fellows."

When we arrived in the kitchen, eight fresh pies were cooling on the kitchen table. Lined up along the counter were jars and jars of canned peaches, and there were more ready to go into the two canners Mamma had boiling on top of the range. The air was thick and hot with steam from the boiling kettles.

"Can the pies be cut yet?" Tom asked.

"They'll be better in another hour or two," Mamma said, "but I reckon you can cut up a few for you boys."

"J.D. will help me carry them out," Tom said.

As I went to our bedroom to get dimes for Frankie and me, I began to wonder if Mamma had any idea Tom was selling pieces of pie to the fellows. I decided she probably didn't, but I was not about to tell her. I am no snitch, and besides, I'd learned a long time ago that it doesn't pay for me to try to outwit Tom.

Tom and I carried pie out to the other boys, then I went back for our pieces. In a short time, all that could be heard was the sound of eating and contented little noises coming from Herbie. He ate all of his pie before anyone else, then licked the plate clean.

Just when Herbie finished licking his plate, Mamma appeared with a pitcher of water.

"Lemonade would be too sour after all that sweetness,"

she said, "but I wonder if any of you young men would care for a drink of nice cool water."

"I would," Parley said.

"Thank you, Ma'am
And my, oh my,
Would you be so kind
As to sell me more pie?" Herbie asked.

Mamma was so startled that she almost dropped the pitcher. "Sell you more pie?" she said. "Why, I sent that pie out to thank you boys for your help."

"I already paid them, ten cents each, for their help," Tom said, smooth as a whistle.

"And then we paid him ten cents each for a piece of pie," Jimmie said.

"He even made me pay ten cents," Frankie said in a quavery voice, "for a piece of my own mamma's pie."

Mamma put the pitcher down on the grass and placed her hands on her hips. It was good that she never scolded us in front of the other kids or Tom's ears would have been blistered right then. Instead she said, "Well, Tom Dennis, you will return those dimes immediately, all of them, including Frankie's and John D.'s."

From the way Mamma called him by his full name, Tom knew not to argue. He gave all us fellows back our money. Then Mamma asked Parley, Herbie, and Jimmie to come with her to the kitchen door. She gave each fellow a pie to take home with him to his family. After that she came back out to the yard where Frankie and I were finishing up our pie and Tom was kicking dirt over the fire under the apple-butter kettle.

"Now, Tom Dennis," she said. "What do you have to say for yourself?"

"Those peaches were mine," Tom said. "Chief Rising Sun sent them to me because I figured out how to prove Henry Martin was lying about the Paiute braves stealing."

"Well, pardon me if I didn't hear correctly," Mamma said. "Perhaps I need my ears cleaned out. John D., tell Tom Dennis exactly what Running Bear said."

"Running Bear told us the Chief sent the peaches as a gift for his friend Fitzgerald," I said.

"Right," Mamma said. "His *friend*. If those peaches had been for you, the Chief would have sent them to his blood brother."

Well, Tom sure couldn't argue with that, because it was the truth. He didn't argue much either when Mamma next told him to pay Frankie and me each ten cents.

"Why?" he asked, sounding astonished.

"Because you are paying boys ten cents each for preparing peaches, so you pay John D. and Frankie too," Mamma said, "unless you wish to have the silent treatment until after you leave for Boylestown."

Tom knew Mamma meant serious business when she mentioned the silent treatment. Mamma and Papa hadn't given any of us the silent treatment in a long time, not since Frankie had run away after it. They'd decided that Sweyn, Tom, and I were too old for it, and that Frankie didn't understand. So when Mamma now threatened the silent treatment, Tom knew he didn't stand a chance. He gave Frankie and me each a dime, and he helped Mamma clean up in the kitchen too.

I was glad to get that money, and I was glad to see Tom's great brain and his money-loving heart swindled at last, and by his own mother. Not that Mamma would ever think she'd swindled Tom, but as far as I was concerned it amounted to the same thing.

But most of all, I was happy that Tom didn't get the silent treatment. Not because it would have been hard on him, but because of Mamma. I knew that she would suffer when Tom and Sweyn left for Boylestown, and I didn't want her to have to send Tom off without saying good-bye. That would have broken Mamma's heart.

Tom spent his last few days at home helping Papa at the *Advocate,* and he spent his last evenings sitting on Polly Reagan's front porch. That had been his pattern for so much of the summer that I didn't realize how much excitement he'd put into those long, hot days until it came time to say good-bye.

I was used to Sweyn being away, but Tom was another matter. As we stood by the big locomotive, waiting for the conductor to shout, "All aboard!" I was plumb sad. For some awful minutes I thought I would embarrass myself and the whole family by bursting into tears.

Then the engine built up a head of steam, and the whistle sounded. Frankie clapped his hands over his ears, but I loved that whistle, even though it meant the train was taking Tom away from me. The locomotive came to life. Its big wheels creaked and the sides of its blue steel belly trembled as if the iron horse couldn't wait to be off down the track.

"All aboard!" shouted the conductor in his deep voice.

Tom kissed Mamma and Aunt Bertha, shook hands with Papa, and swung onto the train before Sweyn even had time to pick up his carpetbag. In another minute both of my older brothers were leaning out the window, waving, and the train was moving off down the track, headed east.

Frankie and I stood looking after the train for a long time. When it was finally out of sight, Frankie put his fists in his eyes and began crying. "I miss T.D. already," he said. "Please, J.D., make the train bring T.D. back."

Maybe I should have been even sadder since Frankie was crying. But I wasn't.

"Don't you worry," I said, putting my arm around his shoulders. "T.D. will be home again. And when he comes home, life will be just as interesting and exciting as it always is with T.D. around. The Great Brain with his money-loving heart will find some way to swindle you and all the other citizens of Adenville."

"Promise?" Frankie said, still rubbing at his eyes.

There was no question about it. I knew the answer as well as I knew my name was John D. Fitzgerald.

"Promise," I said.

KEEP READING FOR A LOOK AT

THE GREAT BRAIN'S VERY FIRST SWINDLE!

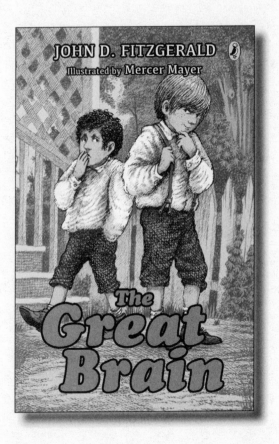

Text copyright © 1969 by John D. Fitzgerald

CHAPTER ONE

The Magic Water Closet

MOST EVERYONE IN UTAH remembers 1896 as the year the territory became a state. But in Adenville it was celebrated by all the kids in town and by Papa and Mamma as the time of The Great Brain's reformation.

I was seven years old going on eight. Tom was ten, and my other brother, Sweyn, would soon be twelve. We were all born and raised in Adenville, which was a typical Utah town with big wide streets lined with trees that had been planted by the early Mormon pioneers.

Adenville had a population of twenty-five hundred people, of which about two thousand were Mormons and the rest Catholics and Protestants. Mormons and non-Mormons had learned to live together with some degree of tolerance and understanding by that time. But tolerance hadn't come easy for my oldest brother, Sweyn, my brother Tom, and myself. Most of our playmates were Mormon kids, but we taught them tolerance. It was just a question of us all learning how to fight good enough for Sweyn to whip every Mormon kid his age, Tom to whip every Mormon kid his age, and for me to whip every Mormon kid my age in town. After all, there is nothing as tolerant and understanding as a kid you can whip.

We never had any really cold weather or snow in Adenville because it was situated in the southwestern part of Utah, known to the Mormons as Dixie due to its mild climate. This was fortunate since we didn't have indoor toilets then. Everybody in town—from Calvin Whitlock, the banker, down—had to use a backhouse until the water closet Papa ordered arrived from Sears Roebuck. We called them backhouses and not outhouses because in Utah an outhouse was a sort of toolshed and storage room. Backhouses ran from two-holers to six-holers. Ours was a standard four-holer. You could just about judge a family's station in life by their backhouse. Just by looking at the Whitlock backhouse, with its ornate scroll woodwork trim and its fancy vent, you knew Calvin Whitlock was a person of means and influence in the community.

If there was one man in all of Adenville who would order the first water closet ever seen in town, that man had to be Papa. I thought Papa was the greatest man in the world except for one weakness. Papa just couldn't resist ordering any new invention that he saw advertised in magazines or catalogs. Our big attic was filled with crazy inventions that didn't work. Papa was always threatening to write to

2

the presidents of these companies and denounce them as swindlers, but he never did. I guess he was afraid they would write back and call him a fool for believing what they said in their advertisements. Papa was editor and publisher of the *Adenville Weekly Advocate*. You would think a man smart enough to be an editor and publisher would be smart enough not to let himself be swindled. But Papa kept right on ordering new inventions. It was no surprise to anybody in town when they learned Papa had ordered the first water closet most people had ever seen.

The first Tom and I knew of it was the morning Fred Harvey walked into our backyard with a pick and shovel on his shoulder. He was the only plumber in town. He was a middle-aged man with a face that looked as if he'd just taken a bite out of a sour pickle. He was known as a very cranky person who didn't like kids. Mamma said the reason Mr. Harvey didn't like kids was because he had never had to put up with any of his own. It didn't sound quite right to me, but that is what Mamma said.

When Mr. Harvey came into our backyard, Tom and I were on our big back porch which ran the width of our house. We were beating with sticks on Mamma's washtubs, pretending that we were drummers in a band. Tom had a grin on his freckled face as he banged away. He was the only one in our family who had freckles. Tom didn't look like Papa and he didn't look like Mamma, unless you put them together. Then you could see that his hair was a cross between Papa's dark hair and Mamma's blond hair and that he had Papa's nose and mouth and Mamma's stubborn chin. Where the freckles came from was a mystery. I took after Papa and had curly black hair and dark eyes. My other brother, Sweyn, took after the Danish grandfather for whom he was named. He had blond hair and a stubborn Danish chin.

Tom and I heard the clanking sound of the pick and shovel being dropped to the ground by Mr. Harvey over the sound of our beating on the washtubs. We stopped and turned around to watch.

Mr. Harvey pulled a bandanna handkerchief from his overalls' pocket and blew his nose loudly. Then he looked at us as if he resented us being on our own back porch.

"Why aren't you kids in school?" he demanded.

"Because there isn't any school today," Tom said, glaring right back at Mr. Harvey. "And there might not be any school for a whole week."

"And why not?" Mr. Harvey asked.

"Because Miss Thatcher is sick," Tom answered.

Mr. Harvey certainly knew that Miss Thatcher taught the first through the sixth grades in our one-room schoolhouse. He also knew that when she was sick there wasn't any school for any kid in town. I guess this kind of upset him.

"If I'd known that," he said as if angry, "I wouldn't have taken this job."

Tom and I watched Mr. Harvey start to dig a hole in our backyard.

"What is he doing?" I asked, just as curious as I could be.

"Let's find out," Tom said.

We left the porch and approached Mr. Harvey.

"Why are you digging a hole?" Tom asked, polite as all get out.

"To bury nosy little boys in," Mr. Harvey said gruffly. "Now get away from me and leave me to my work."

"Come on, J.D.," Tom said, heading back for the porch. "We'll ask Mamma."

4

My brothers and I always called each other by our initials because that was the way Papa addressed us. We all had the same middle initial because we all had the same middle name of Dennis, just like Papa. More than two hundred years before I was born, an ancestor of ours named Dennis betrayed six of his cousins to the English during the rebellion in County Meath, Ireland. His father decreed that all male Fitzgeralds must bear the middle name of Dennis to remind them of the cowardice of his son.

I followed Tom into our big kitchen with its ten-foot-wide coal-burning range. Mamma was kneading dough on the big kitchen table as we entered. I had never seen Mamma's hands idle. They were busy hands—sewing, mending, cooking, washing, knitting, and always moving.

Mamma's blond hair was piled high in braids on her head. The sunshine coming through the kitchen window and striking Mamma's head made her hair look like golden sunlight.

She looked at us and smiled. "What have you two boys on your minds?" she asked.

"Why is Mr. Harvey digging a hole in our backyard?" Tom asked.

"It is the cesspool for the water closet your father ordered from Sears Roebuck," Mamma answered.

Aunt Bertha, who had lived with us since the death of her husband, was greasing a bread pan with bacon rinds. She wasn't really our aunt, but we called her Aunt Bertha because she was just like one of the family.

"This water closet business is the most foolish thing your husband ever did," she said to Mamma. When Aunt Bertha criticized Papa, he was always Mamma's "husband." When Papa did something Aunt Bertha approved of, he became "that man of ours." She was a big woman, with hands and feet like a man's and gray hair she always wore in a bun at the nape of her neck.

Tom scratched his freckled nose as wrinkles appeared on his high forehead. "You put china in a china closet," he said slowly. "You put clothes in a clothes closet. You put linen in a linen closet. But how can you put water in a water closet?"

I was dumbfounded. It was the first time in my life I'd ever heard my brother, with his great brain, admit he didn't know everything. Every year when Papa renewed his subscription to the *New York World,* they sent him *The World Almanac.* While Sweyn and I read books like *Black Beauty* and *Huckleberry Finn,* Tom read *The World Almanac* and the set of encyclopedias in our bookcase. Tom said his great brain had to know everything.

"A water closet is a toilet you have inside your house," Mamma explained. "That is why your father had Mr. Jamison partition off that room in the bathroom. The hole Mr. Harvey is digging is the cesspool for the new water closet."

"But Mamma," I protested, thinking about the odor coming from our backhouse, especially on hot days, "it will stink up the whole house."

Aunt Bertha agreed with me. "I tell you, Tena," she said to Mamma, "this is going to make us the laughing stock of Adenville."

"Now, Bertha," Mamma said with soft rebuke, "I've seen water closets in hotels in Salt Lake City and in Denver while on my honeymoon. I assure you they are very convenient and sanitary."

I remembered how I couldn't believe you could get water without a pump until they built the Adenville reser-

6

voir and Papa had explained how the reservoir being on higher ground forced the water through the pipes. And when Mr. Harvey had installed our hot-water heater and we got hot water right out of a tap, I thought it a miracle. But a backhouse in our bathroom was beyond my wildest imagination. I was positive that Papa had been swindled again on another crazy invention.

Tom and I went back outside to the porch. We watched as Mr. Harvey continued to dig the cesspool. In a little while Sammy Leeds, Danny Forester, and Andy Anderson came into our backyard. Mr. Harvey chased them away and told them to stay out of the backyard while he was working. Tom and I sat on the porch, watching until lunchtime.

Papa came home for lunch with Sweyn, who had been helping at the newspaper office. Mr. Harvey came to our back door. He demanded that Papa keep all kids out of the backyard while he was working. Papa told Sweyn to remain home to see that this was done.

"Can we watch from the back porch?" Tom asked.

"Yes," Papa agreed, "but stay out of the yard."

I could tell from the conniving look on Tom's face during lunch that his great brain was working like sixty to turn this to his financial advantage. He disappeared right after lunch. I went out to the back porch with Sweyn.

Mr. Harvey had just finished eating his own lunch which he had brought in a shoebox. He went to the hydrant and got a drink of water and then went to work. Mamma had asked him to have lunch with us, but Mr. Harvey had refused.

Sweyn and I sat on the railing of the back porch watching.

"Think you'll have any fights keeping the kids out of the backyard?" I asked hopefully.

7

"There is nobody left to fight," Sweyn said as if he regretted it.

"Maybe when Papa and Mamma send you to Salt Lake City to school next fall, you'll find some kids there to fight," I said, wanting to cheer him up.

He shook his head sadly. "It's a Catholic academy, J.D., and I don't believe the sisters or priests who teach there will allow any fighting."

I thought ahead to the time when I would be graduating from the sixth grade in Adenville like Sweyn would in June of that year. I too would be sent to school in Salt Lake City. The thought scared me and made my mouth dry. I went into the kitchen to get a drink of water, just as the door leading to our side porch was thrust open. I stared bug-eyed as I watched Tom come through the hallway that separated our kitchen and dining room, followed by ten kids.

"It is all right, Mamma," Tom said as if he led ten kids into our kitchen every day. "Papa ordered Sweyn to keep the kids out of the backyard while Mr. Harvey is digging. But Papa said it was all right to watch from the porch. We can't get to the back porch without going into the backyard unless we go through the kitchen."

Aunt Bertha shook her head. "I tell you, Tena, that boy could talk his way around anything."

"He gets it from his father," Mamma said as if she was proud of Tom instead of angry with him for marching ten kids across her clean kitchen floor.

I couldn't believe my eyes as I watched Mamma go into the pantry and return with a big crock jar filled with cookies. She stationed herself near the door leading to the back porch.

"All right, boys," she said, smiling, "help yourselves to an oatmeal cookie as you pass by."

I had to fall in line last to get one of my own mother's cookies. Tom was munching on his cookie as I joined him on the back porch.

"You know, J.D.," he said as he finished the last bite of his cookie and folded his arms on his chest, "there is room for at least ten more kids on this porch. I am going to give you an opportunity to share in this business venture of mine."

"Business venture?" I asked, not knowing what he meant. "What business venture?"

"You didn't think I let these kids see the digging of the first cesspool in Adenville for nothing, did you?" he asked as if I'd insulted him. "I charged them a penny apiece. You go round up ten more kids. Tell them they not only get to see the digging of the first cesspool for a water closet for a penny, but also that they will be served refreshments. Collect the money in advance. No credit or promises."

"How do you know Mamma will give them a cookie?" I asked.

"She has to," Tom said confidently, "because she gave all the other kids a cookie."

"What do I get out of it?" I asked. I knew from past experience that it always pays to spell out the terms when making a business deal with my brother.

"I'll pay you a commission of one penny for each five kids," Tom answered. "If you round up ten more kids, you will make two cents."

How proud I was a half hour later as I marched ten kids into our kitchen and told them to line up to receive one of Mamma's delicious oatmeal cookies. Mamma's attitude puzzled me. She didn't look pleased and proud as she had with Tom. I caught her giving me a funny look as she held the cookie jar and each kid helped himself to a cookie.

I was at the end of the line and all set to have another cookie when Mamma snapped the lid back on the jar.

"You had a cookie, John D.," she said. "Please inform Tom D. the cookie jar is empty. I wasn't prepared to serve cookies to every boy in town."

I thought Mr. Harvey would be mad as all get out at having twenty kids watching him. But as the afternoon wore on he seemed to like playing to an audience, especially when he hit a big rock which he had to lift out of the hole. It was a heavy rock for one man to lift. All the kids applauded. Mr. Harvey looked at us and appeared to almost, but not quite, smile.

When Mr. Harvey quit work that day, he told Mamma to tell Papa that it would take two more days to finish the cesspool.

"Did you hear that, J.D.," Tom said, rubbing his hands together. "I knew my great brain would make me a fortune some day. Twenty kids tomorrow and twenty more the day after. That adds up to forty cents."

"How about me?" I asked, not wanting to be frozen out of this financial bonanza.

"I'm sorry, J.D.," he said, patting my shoulder, "but you know what Mamma said about the cookie jar. That means I'll have to buy some gingersnaps myself to serve as refreshments."

The next morning I went with Tom to Zion's Cooperative Mercantile Institution, which was the name given to stores all over Utah which were owned by the Mormon Church. There was one in every town, and you could buy anything from a penny stick of licorice to a plow and harrow in them. Most people simply called them the Z.C.M.I. store,

10

although some Mormons did call them the Co-op. Tom bought a five-cent box of gingersnaps which contained twenty cookies.

Mr. Harvey played to a full house for the next two days. He finished digging the hole, which was over ten feet deep and about ten feet across, and a trench two feet deep and about a foot and a half wide that ran from the hole right under our house where the bathroom was located. Then he brought a wagonload of cedar posts which he used to line the sides of the cesspool, tying them together with baling wire. He also brought clay pipe, which he laid in the trench, and filled the joints with mortar. Then he covered the cesspool with cedar posts and boards over which he put two feet of dirt. He filled the trench with dirt, covering up the clay pipes just as the day's work finished.

Mamma must have felt a little guilty about not serving the kids cookies for those two days because she made lemonade for all the kids both days. Tom of course took all the credit, saying the lemonade was included in the price of admission. His great brain had made him a fortune in three days.

The failure of the new inventions Papa ordered was always made all the more embarrassing because he bragged about them in advance. The water closet was no exception. Everybody in town knew about it long before it arrived.

Nels Larson was stationmaster, ticket agent, telegrapher, express agent, and freight agent at the railroad depot. He never delivered any express or freight except the things Papa ordered. Mr. Larson would simply telephone people and tell them they had express or freight shipments at the depot and to come and get them. But his curiosity always got the best of him when anything came for Papa. When the

11

water closet arrived, he went home and got his own team and wagon to make the delivery. He told his wife the water closet had come. Mrs. Larson got right on the telephone to spread the news all over town.

By the time Mr. Larson had returned to the depot and loaded the crates containing the water closet, his wife had let everybody know that today was the day. Mr. Larson was a middle-aged man with blond hair and a light complexion stemming from his Swedish heritage. He always walked leaning forward as if walking into a strong wind and rode on the seat of his wagon the same way. He drove the team from the depot right down Main Street, with people leaving their places of business and homes to follow him. When he stopped in front of our house, there were about two hundred men, women, and children in the street. Mamma took one look out the bay window in the parlor and telephoned Papa at the *Advocate* office. Mr. Larson was poised over a wooden crate with a hammer in his right hand, right in the middle of Main Street, when Papa arrived.

"What in the name of Jupiter do you think you are doing?" Papa demanded. "Make the delivery in the rear."

"Nothing in the rules, Fitz, says I've got to make deliveries in the rear," Mr. Larson said.

"You don't have to open the crates right in the middle of Main Street," Papa said.

"Rules and regulations say I've got to inspect the merchandise for damage," Mr. Larson said.

"You know very well, Nels," Papa said testily, "the only time you ever inspect anything is when the shipment is for me."

"Ain't nothing interesting in the others," Mr. Larson said.

12

"Now you listen to me, Nels," Papa said, his dark eyes flaming with anger. "I will not permit you to make a spectacle of my water closet in the middle of Main Street."

"And you listen to me, Fitz," Mr. Larson said, pointing his hammer at Papa. "It is my job to inspect the merchandise for damage and that is just what I intend to do. Don't want you blaming the railroad or the express company because this crazy contraption doesn't work."

"What makes you so certain it won't work?" Papa asked, glaring at the stationmaster.

"None of those other new-fangled inventions you ordered worked," Mr. Larson answered, putting Papa in his place.

"Go ahead and open it," Papa said in complete defeat.

The first crate Mr. Larson opened contained the copper-lined water tank, which he placed on exhibition on top of the crate. He stepped back and eyed it critically.

"Can't figure out what that is for," he said.

"Are you satisfied it isn't damaged?" Papa said as if trying to control his temper. "If so, I assure you that Mr. Harvey and I will know what it is for." Then Papa folded his arms on his chest like a martyr. "Since you are bound and determined to hold a public unveiling of my water closet in the middle of Main Street, please get on with it."

"No reason to get sore," Mr. Larson said indignantly, "just because a man is doing his job according to the rules and regulations."

The next crate contained the big brass pipe that we later learned connected the water tank near the ceiling to the bowl on the floor. Mr. Larson held it up as if it were a spyglass.

"You've been swindled again," he said to Papa as he laid the pipe down.

Papa was positively fuming as Mr. Larson opened the next crate which contained the porcelain bowl. Mr. Larson placed it like a trophy on top of the crate for all to see.

"It is beginning to make sense," Mr. Larson had to admit, "but that bowl is plumb too big for kids."

"Just determine if it is damaged and get on with it," Papa said, so angry he turned his back on Mr. Larson.

It wasn't until the stationmaster removed the wooden toilet seat that his skepticism began to vanish. He held it in front of his face as if it were a picture frame, as he slowly turned around for all to see.

"This is the thing-a-mah-bob you sit on!" he shouted as if making a great discovery.

There were many *ohs* and *ahs* from the crowd who were used to sitting on boards with holes cut in them.

Papa then sent me to fetch Mr. Harvey. I thought from the way Papa's jaws were puffed up that he would explode before I returned with the plumber, but he didn't. Mr. Harvey and I arrived just as the public unveiling of our water closet on Main Street came to a close.

Mr. Harvey pushed Mr. Larson to one side and began searching through the crates until he found a big brown envelope containing the instructions for assembling the water closet. Then his and Papa's troubles began. Every man, woman, and child who could get their hands on any part of the water closet as it was being carried to our bathroom thought their help entitled them to remain and watch it being assembled.

"Make everybody clear out of here," Mr. Harvey said to Papa as he plunked his tool case down on the bathroom floor. "Can't do a blooming thing with all these people hanging around in here."

14

Papa asked everybody to leave. Nobody budged an inch until Papa promised they could all see the water closet and how it worked after it was assembled. He even made Sweyn, Tom, and me leave.

The crowd broke up into small groups in our backyard and on our front lawn. They spoke in hushed whispers as people do at funerals. I wandered from group to group, listening. The more I listened, the more humiliated I became.

"Wouldn't want one of those things in my house," I heard Dave Teller, the shoemaker, telling a small group. "It is bound to stink up the whole house."

"Not only the house," Mr. Carter, who worked at the creamery, said, "but the whole neighborhood if that cesspool caves in during a rain storm."

My friend Howard Kay didn't help matters as he sidled up to me as if ashamed of being seen with me.

"Gosh, John," he whispered, "folks are saying your pa has gone plumb loco putting a backhouse in your bathroom." He put his fingers to his nose. "Phewee! I'd hate to be living in your house."

It was too much for me. I held back tears of humiliation until I'd run upstairs to the room I shared with Tom. I flung myself on the bed and began to cry. I had always been proud of Papa in spite of him buying crazy inventions that didn't work. But this time he'd gone too far. He had done what Aunt Bertha said he would do. He had made us Fitzgeralds the laughing stock of Adenville. Nobody would come to our house anymore. How could Mamma entertain the Ladies Sewing Circle in a house that smelled like a backhouse? It would be the same as entertaining in our old backhouse. I visualized callers at our house stopping at the front gate and putting clothespins on their noses before entering our home.

15

I don't know for how long I lay there crying with shame before I heard a terrifying clanging and banging as if somebody had dropped a lot of pans and kettles off our roof. I dropped to my knees. I was positive the water closet had exploded.

"Please, God, spare my Papa," I prayed.

Then I ran downstairs. I expected to find Mamma hysterical with grief and Papa and Mr. Harvey blown to kingdom come. Instead I found Mamma and Aunt Bertha in the kitchen making plattersful of sandwiches. I ran into the bathroom. Papa and Mr. Harvey were standing looking at the installed water closet with smug expressions on their faces. The porcelain bowl was bolted to the floor in one corner of the room that had been partitioned off. The wooden seat had been attached to it. The water tank was fastened to the wall near the ceiling, with a water pipe running up to it. The big brass pipe was connected to the water tank and the bowl. There was a brass chain attached to the water tank, with a wooden handle on it.

"One more time to make sure," Papa said to Mr. Harvey.

I watched Mr. Harvey pull on the chain. There was a clanging sound and then water rushed down the brass pipe from the water tank into the porcelain bowl, filling it up, and then suddenly the water in the bowl disappeared.

"She is ready and rarin' to go," Mr. Harvey said, and for the first time in my life I saw him smile.

It was surely a miracle invention, but there was one thing I had to know.

"Will it stink?" I asked.

"No, J.D.," Papa answered. "The water level in the bowl will keep any air or odor from coming up from the cesspool."